A SUITABLE

COMPANION

FOR THE END

OF YOUR

LIFE

A SUITABLE

COMPANION

FOR THE END

OF YOUR

LIFE

ROBERT MCGILL

COACH HOUSE BOOKS, TORONTO

first edition

Published with the generous assistance of the Canada Council for the Arts and the Ontario Arts Council. Coach House Books also acknowledges the support of the Government of Canada through the Canada Book Fund and the Government of Ontario through the Ontario Book Publishing Tax Credit.

LIBRARY AND ARCHIVES CANADA CATALOGUING IN PUBLICATION

Title: A suitable companion for the end of your life / Robert McGill.
Names: McGill, Robert, author.
Identifiers: Canadiana (print) 20210387106 | Canadiana (ebook) 20210387114 | ISBN 9781552454442 (softcover) | ISBN 9781770567191 (PDF) | ISBN 9781770567184 (EPUB)
Classification: LCC PS8625.G54 S85 2022 | DDC C813/.6—dc23

A Suitable Companion for the End of Your Life is available as an ebook: ISBN 978 1 77056 718 4 (EPUB), ISBN 978 1 77056 719 1 (PDF)

Purchase of the print version of this book entitles you to a free digital copy. To claim your ebook of this title, please email sales@chbooks.com with proof of purchase. (Coach House Books reserves the right to terminate the free digital download offer at any time.)

for Fiona

Who has turned us around so that,
whatever we do, we have the bearing
of one going away? As on that last
hill, which shows him his valley
a final time, he turns, halts, lingers –
that's how we live, always saying goodbye.

– Rainer Maria Rilke, *Duino Elegies*

ONE

ÜLLE

Regan decided that living wasn't for her, maybe. There was no Hail Mary left or last ditch, just misery on misery. Lucinda ghosting her. A stress fracture that wouldn't heal. Parents absent without leave. The final college rejection letter sat on the kitchen table, last in a line of terse, nearly identical quasi-apologies: *A deep pool of applications this year, more excellent candidates than places, please don't take it personally and do something we'll all regret.* Words along those lines anyhow, as if the admissions officer felt terrible, wasn't just feeding her copypasta. As if things had truly nearly worked out.

She spent her days alone in the house. The track team had forgotten her. Nobody at the store except Paul seemed to care that she'd quit, and she was sick of hearing from him. It had been a lousy job, shoddy hours, a summer gig stretched into fake full-time. She was eighteen and nowhere. Online, she researched flatpacks. Half a dozen times, she almost went for it. Then came a Sunday when her mother didn't bother to call. Ten minutes a week telling Regan about all the busyness at work had become too much to ask. A proper family would have been finishing dinner together when Regan phoned the consulate in Auckland, where it was already Monday morning, and listened to her mother's secretary ask if the situation was urgent.

'Never mind,' said Regan. 'You've been a big help.'

'Are you all right?' the secretary asked, as though just then realizing that Regan might not be. When hiring staff, her mother had once told her, choose IQ over empathy. Regan hung up.

She would have called her father, but the treatment centre had a policy and she didn't want to trigger him, so she laced up her running shoes, striking a deal with herself. If she could manage a single pain-free mile, she wouldn't place the order.

Outside, the first ten steps felt how a run was supposed to feel, unfettered, loping, legs light as milkweed gone to fluff. There was only a little dizziness from skipping lunch. In her mind, she was already blocks away, running across the pedestrian bridge into the park, when her foot burst into its familiar agony. She hopped to a standstill, not even out of the cul-de-sac. Then she limped back to the house.

That night, with her dinner of Special K uneaten, the dregs of a wine bottle silty in her glass, and the final purchase page aglow on her phone, she had an urge to see whether her parents were somehow upstairs in their bed, magically returned without telling her. The last rejection letter still sat on the table, stuffed back into its envelope. Her running shoes lay flopped against each other in the corner. When she'd flung them there, she hadn't seen Toodles camped over the heating grate. Now he refused to come when she called, when she sobbed apologies, when she rained cat kibble into his bowl from knee height to maximize the clatter, then mimed eating the stuff to make him jealous.

'Mmmm,' she said, down on her hands and knees. 'So good.' The fish-meal smell turned her stomach, and it occurred to her that she was drunk.

On her phone, she accepted the terms and conditions. The screen froze, for sure a sign that her mother's credit card was maxing out, but then the transaction went through. Regan called for Toodles. He didn't show. Descending to her mother's basement office, she printed the declaration from the website, scrawled a signature that looked like a crude forgery of her own, and left the sheet on the desk for the cops to find. A second later, her kilter went from under her. Her fall was broken by the floor. She crawled toward the stairs and almost made it before passing out.

When she woke, she stumbled up to bed, leaving all the lights in the house blazing.

The doorbell gonged at noon. The night had been real; the ringing and her hangover were hard proof. She went downstairs determined not to wuss out, her brain a blister on the verge of popping.

No one stood at the door or in the driveway. There was only a box on the step, tall as her waist and hardly wider, plain brown cardboard without logo or address. Not cool that they'd just abandoned the thing when the website had made such a big deal about secrecy.

The lack of heft as she lifted the box over the threshold was weird. She set it in the living room, then went around the house closing blinds and curtains, sealing the doors and windows with masking tape. There was no sign of Toodles, and the kibble in his bowl sat untouched. Out on a hunting trip, probably. It had been yonks since his last murdered chickadee, but venturing outside let him pretend he still had the chops. Regan went to the mudroom and closed the latch on the cat flap, feeling guilty for not saying goodbye. Now his last memory of her wouldn't be her stomach's heat as the two of them curled on the couch together; it was going to be her shoes, hurtling toward him with rubbery fury. He'd never know that she'd just saved his life.

In the living room, she still wasn't ready to face the box, so she checked her phone. Paul had left a long voice mail about the power of accepting people's love that she deleted halfway through. Then she saw that Lucinda had texted. Her heart did a pirouette, until she realized that all Lucinda had written was '*Thinking ofu.*' For some reason, Regan's first assumption was that Lucinda had meant to type '*Thinking tofu.*' Which didn't make much sense.

The box's flaps were covered with layers of packing tape, so she retrieved the bread knife from the kitchen and sliced along the creases. After opening one end, she tipped the box onto its side and reached in. There'd been videos of people doing this, back before their relatives had got the clips taken down, back when there was a sick giddiness in witnessing the people's ignorance of what was to come. She'd never managed to watch past this point in the proceedings: the box open, the package pulled out.

It was tubular and wrapped in clear plastic, like a chub of ground beef. What it held looked like a rolled-up rug, except the rug had a silvery tint and the smoothness of uncooked chicken. Also, the near end wasn't a textile whorl; it was a flattened pair of human feet.

She bent to examine their snaky veins, their unvarnished nails, the eddying prints on the tiptoes like the patterns that waves leave in sand. The feet lay sandwiched between the wrapping on one side and the rolled-up legs attached to them on the other, their heels deflated, the pancaked flesh spreading from ankles that had been folded forward to a boneless angle.

Regan fingered the wrapping and felt no warmth. She rolled the package across the carpet, inspecting it as she went. The knees aligned neatly with one another, the skin there thickly ribbed. Her eyes scanned upward along the backs of the thighs until she realized what came next and grew flushed. By the time she turned the thing further, her forehead pricked with sweat, but she only found herself back at the feet, curiosity rebuffed by the roll's tight coil.

Now was when things were supposed to start their end. One slice of the knife and she'd have just a few days left to live. She thought of calling Lucinda and letting her know, asking whether she still thought of Regan as a survivor who would do fine on her own, if she still believed that the stress fracture was bound to heal, if she was still so sure that a college would write with good news.

Across the room, a whole shelf of the built-in bookcase lay empty. Her father had insisted on taking way too many books with him to the treatment centre. Philosophy books and meditation books and books about sustainable living. Books with titles that told you to take six steps toward self-care, think like a puppy, or unfreeze your inner caveman. Books that promised to change your life. He seldom actually read them, but he liked to leave them around the house like a squirrel stashing nuts, nervous about future need.

Regan's head felt too heavy to hold up. All her life, she'd tried to be a good person. She hadn't read all the self-help books either, but she'd worked hard chasing happiness, maybe harder than her father had. Other people didn't need to put in such an effort. They made it seem like happiness was an easy night together, like you could just text 'u up?' and happiness would come over, like it wouldn't slap you when you tried to hold its hand. Didn't she deserve a bit of that? If not true happiness, then at least a few days of induced contentment. Someone to take care of her, make her feel good at the end, just by being there. Never mind that it was all chimerical. At this point, she'd take even a chemical miracle.

She didn't bother with the bread knife; she dug into the package's plastic sheathing with her fingernails. It stretched but refused to break, until she had a thick wad in her fist and a long strip dangled like a tendon of clear taffy. Finally, it snapped off without even the satisfaction of a noise. She plunged her face into the hole she'd made and huffed, wanting the buzz that people raved about – the few who'd felt it and lived. The tide surge of tranquility through your pleasure centre, the deepening acceptance of your place in the universe that made every subsequent thing seem fine. Snatching the air through her nostrils, she expected some beautiful sham of an aroma, like lime and cedar shavings with vanilla drizzle, candle-grade fakery masking the odour of bleach or bitter almonds. Instead, she smelled something like mown grass.

The surprise of it gave her pause. Maybe she was making a mistake. She was so good at making them. It might not be too late. She could patch the hole, call 911, drive herself to an emergency room, let the cops in their hazmat suits deal with the disposal.

Maybe it wouldn't mean jail. They might just put her in some place like the one her father was in.

No, that was the coward in her talking. She'd made her choice.

With the knife, she sawed at the sheathing until the roll inside seemed to strain against its imprisonment. When she split the plastic, the roll sprang out and unfurled with an oomph of pent-up force, splaying on its front across the floor.

Now there was no avoiding the butt. It lay flanked by hips that flared wide as jodhpurs. The skin wore a silver sheen, like it had been shellacked. The shoulder blades were little more than dimples, the neck seemed barely there, and the head had the flatness of a ping-pong paddle, with red hair cropped as short as the real grass in ritzy mini-golf. The face was hidden from her, pressed into the carpet.

At the top of the neck, behind the left ear, just where it was supposed to be, protruded a black metal spigot, not much bigger than the nozzle on water wings. When Regan leaned down to put her lips around it, she tasted ChapStick and couldn't tell if it was the spigot's own flavour or the leftovers from someone's mouth. Blowing three long breaths, she saw no rise in the chest, no ballooning of the fingers; she only heard a faint, dispersive whiffle from invisible pores. She kept on blowing until there was a string of little pops, like knuckles being cracked. Then, out of nowhere, a clod of pleasure walloped her skull, not like the buzz she'd read about, but like a packet of sweetness bursting. It hadn't yet subsided when a stream of sick welled up in her. She made it to the toilet just in time.

The sickness felt like punishment for the pleasure, even though blowing was what you were supposed to do. She told herself this, but a lingering guilt made her reluctant to re-enter the living room. Anyway, the website had said it would take a few hours for the blowing to take effect, and it seemed creepy just to wait around getting high off a flat body, so she slid under the quilt in her bedroom and cupped her phone, wondering what to look at. She'd read pretty much everything there was about flatpacks. She didn't want to deal with world or local news. She was done with memes. She searched for 'websites to visit if you have seventy-two hours to live' and was appalled that nothing came up. It seemed to break a fundamental rule of the internet. Then she typed 'cool websites' into the search bar, and by five o'clock she was reading an article titled 'How to Plant Ideas in Someone's Mind' without a clue how she'd got there.

The phone rang and made her jump. It was Paul. She didn't answer. Five minutes passed before a voice mail notification popped up. She listened to a minute of him banging on about some homeopathic treatment for stress fractures he'd seen online, maybe it was bullshit but you never knew, et cetera, until he starting sharing his thoughts on the importance of allowing yourself to be vulnerable with people who loved you, at which point she hit Delete and swiped over to Lucinda's last text again. '*Thinking ofu.*' She thumbed out a reply, '*thinking tofu too,*' wondering whether Lucinda would get the joke.

As she mulled over whether to send it, a high-pitched squalling came from downstairs. In horror, she leapt out of bed, knowing the sound. Toodles, inside the house. He must have been hiding all along.

She found him pacing the living room, yowling, back arched and fur electrically on end.

'Christ,' she whispered. The website had been clear: once the package was open, you weren't allowed to unseal the house. As Toodles twitched and hissed, she began to weep. She tried to tell herself that he was old, it was his time anyway.

'What's wrong?' she asked him through her sniffles. 'What's got into you?'

Toodles wouldn't look at her; his gaze was locked in the direction of the kitchen. Then she realized that the two of them were alone in the living room. The body on the floor had disappeared. A moment later, a groan came from the kitchen.

The body lay collapsed across the breakfast table, fingers gripping its edge, elbows bent as if in an effort to right itself. It had filled out a little, doubling down on its woman's hips. Regan went over and reached beneath the armpits, grasped the shoulders, and felt their lack of heat, their playdough give. Hooking the nearest chair's leg with a foot, she drew it closer, then lowered the woman to let her sit. The woman slumped and gave another groan, wheezing like air was a problem she was working on.

Her face had the features of someone old, though exactly how old Regan couldn't tell, because the wrinkles were in the wrong places, not pinched around the eyelids or crevassing her brow but running vertically from her chin to her squashed forehead. Her lips were bloodless, her nose less a nose than a cratered belly button. Her eyes were closed tight. She had dark eyebrows that arched as though she found the situation puzzling, while her head lolled on her neck like a sunflower loaded with seeds. Regan lay a finger on the woman's throat and felt a syncopated pulse. She leaned her ear close to the mouth and felt feeble breaths. Looking down, she saw the fleshy mud flaps of the woman's breasts and four small scratches on her side from Toodles's claws. Blood beaded at the edges of the torn skin, glistening not red but forest green.

Regan swore and hurried to the bathroom for a roll of gauze. Returning, she cut a swatch to dress the wound. When she'd finished, she stepped back to appraise what she'd done. The patch job somehow accentuated the fact that the woman was naked.

'I didn't buy you clothes,' Regan murmured. She'd never even considered buying them. It would be only a few days, but she should have bought her clothes.

The woman, eyes still shut, gave another groan. 'Hunnn,' she said. 'Hunnnnnn.'

'Hungry?' said Regan. 'Do you need to eat?'

From the fridge she pulled out a carton of apple juice, an orange, and the Tupperware full of quinoa salad she'd kept meaning to eat. From the cupboard she retrieved a pack of rice cakes and the jar of almond butter. The website had claimed that total decompression would take a day or so, but the woman's belly-button nose had already blown up into an outie. The wrinkles on her face were getting shallower. She didn't seem that old now, maybe in her thirties. Her eyes had opened, too, and they followed Regan as she shuttled the food from countertop to table.

'Any of this stuff look good to you?' Regan asked.

The woman's gaze settled on the apple juice, so Regan poured a glass and carried it over, brought it to the woman's mouth, and trickled a bit in. A pale yellow bubble formed between the woman's lips, then swelled and ruptured, and the juice ran back out of her, dribbling down her chin. Her face still held its quizzical expression. Regan grabbed a dishcloth to sop up the mess before she tried again.

It took half an hour to get a glassful down her. The whole time, Regan stayed close by, inhaling deeply, waiting for the buzz to kick in but feeling nothing. Maybe it was too soon. She didn't know what she'd do if the promised blissfulness turned out to be bunk, a lie to let people think that death by flatpack wasn't as gruesome as it seemed.

Toodles mewed from the living room. After a few minutes he stopped, then started again, this time from upstairs. She considered earplugs but instead poured herself a glass of wine and took a slug for every sip of juice she offered her companion. The woman didn't say a word, only gurgled from her throat and, eventually, from her guts. The air around her gained a greenish tinge, and the cut-grass odour of her grew more pungent, while her eyes acquired a glassy, sated look. Regan still didn't feel a buzz. The woman looked even younger now. Late twenties, tops.

'Luh,' she said when the glass was empty. 'Ooh-luh. Ooooh-luh.'

'Ooh-luh?' said Regan. 'Is that your name?' There'd been an Ülle in Grade 12 chemistry, an exchange student from Slovakia, blond and standoffish or maybe just shy. The teacher had made a fool of himself by teasing her all the time. He'd even joked that her family must have got flatpacked. Regan had been just about to rat him out to the principal when the government changed the immigration laws and all the exchange students were sent home.

The woman at the table didn't answer Regan's question. There was only the splatter of something hitting the floor in a stream. At first Regan thought that the woman had knocked over the juice. Then she realized.

'Oh,' she said. 'Okay.'

By the time she'd dragged her to the bathroom, it was pretty much too late. Regan left her sitting on the toilet while she went for the mop and pail. After she finished cleaning the kitchen floor, she returned to the bathroom and found the woman still on the toilet, face buried in her hands. Her neck had to be working better now, because she raised her head to stare at Regan. She looked nearly puffed out to personhood, a body with mass and muscles. Her mouth stretched into a smile.

'Mama,' she said, reaching out her arms. 'Mama!'

'Not Mama,' said Regan. 'Regan.' There was barely time to register the woman's cool, plasticky hands on hers before she was pulled close and the woman's cheek pressed into her midriff. Regan found herself looking down at another person's backside and worrying about the flab on her own belly. It didn't matter how many crunches you did if you never got to run.

'Mama!' the woman said again.

'I'm not your mother,' Regan insisted, pulling away. 'Do you understand what I'm saying? Do you speak English?' In all her reading about flatpacks, she'd never thought about whether they were required to know the language.

'Eng-lish,' the woman repeated, brow furrowing. 'Speak. Little.'

'My name is Ree-gan,' said Regan loudly. 'What's yours?'

The furrow in the woman's brow deepened. 'Mama,' she said without conviction.

'No, what's your name? What are you called? Ülle?' Regan didn't expect her to remember. They weren't supposed to remember anything. But they weren't supposed to call you Mama either.

'Ülle,' the woman said, like it was a question. 'Ülle.'

'All right,' said Regan. 'That's what we'll say it is.'

Ülle still wasn't wearing any clothes. Regan eyeballed her and decided that her own things would be too small.

'I need to go upstairs,' Regan said. 'Stay here, okay?'

Slowly, with little jerks of her chin, as though she were falling asleep, Ülle lowered her head and buried her face in her hands again. She didn't look like she was going anywhere.

In her parents' closet, Regan pilfered a pair of jeans and a sweatshirt from her mother's side. She was about to take them downstairs when she heard Toodles mewing from her bedroom. If he kept this up, she didn't know how she'd get through the next few days. Maybe she could smuggle him out through the cat flap without anyone noticing. The flatpack dealer hadn't been around that long, as far as the people on Regan's favoured discussion boards could tell, and everything about the dealer's website, from the bad grammar to the extensive use of all caps, suggested a small operation. Even if the dealer had somebody staking out the house 24-7, they couldn't keep their eyes on the backyard every minute, could they?

Then she imagined her toenails being prised off, one by one. Her fingernails. Her fingers.

She was such a chicken. The dealer would know it, too, because if she were brave, she wouldn't need Ülle in the first place. Flatpacks were the way out for wimps who couldn't handle a little pain.

Toodles fell silent, and the silence was worse than his mewing. In her room, she found him lying on the bed. He was licking himself frantically, his fur coming off in tufts, exposing patches of pink skin.

Her stomach spasmed. It had happened to him so quickly, and it looked like he wasn't feeling the buzz either. She didn't understand; they'd said it was like being rocked to sleep, like the mellowest dope you'd ever smoke.

She scooped him up and cradled him, stroked him between the ears. He struggled so much to be free that on the way downstairs she almost let go, but she managed to keep hold until reaching the back door, where she undid the latch on the cat flap and shoved him through. She didn't care what the punishment would be. You didn't need all ten fingers anyhow, especially once you were dead.

'Goodbye,' she whispered. 'I'm sorry!' Crouching to peer out after him, she saw only the concrete steps, a stretch of lawn. Then she refastened the latch.

Back in her parents' room to fetch the clothes, she pulled up her top in front of the mirror. No rash or lesions. When she yanked at her hair, it stayed in her head. Maybe Toodles's size had made him more susceptible, or maybe it was because he groomed himself so much. She licked her wrist to see if she could taste greenness there, a spritz of dandelion, but there was only the sour salt of unshowered skin.

'You have many reasons not to kill yourself,' her therapist had said three days earlier.

'Like what?' she'd asked him.

'That's a great question to discuss,' he'd replied, and she'd scowled. It was his policy not to hand out answers, fine, but she didn't consider it professional to withhold a patient's reasons for living.

After all the hints she'd dropped, he should have known that she was thinking of buying a flatpack, but he didn't say anything. Maybe he hadn't heard about the black market and didn't realize that buying flatpacks was a thing you could do. Maybe he just didn't want to validate her latest bag of crazy. Whatever his strategy, he was off his game that day. Didn't bother with his usual mansplaining about her primal wounds. Didn't ask to see her food diary. Maybe he sensed that it was their last session and he was counting down the clock. At the end, he didn't even hug her when she said goodbye. She disliked hugs, but she'd never told him that, not in three years of spilling her guts to him.

When she returned to the downstairs bathroom, she found Ülle contemplating her own fingers, scrunching them into fists and spreading them apart.

'Think you can stand?' said Regan. 'I've got clothes for you.'

Ülle put her hands on the sides of the toilet seat and tried to raise herself, but she succeeded only in scooching forward.

'Can you lift your arms, at least?' Regan said.

In the end, she had to lift each of Ülle's arms for her and work them through the sleeves. Then she pulled the sweatshirt down over Ülle's head.

'Mama, is dark,' said Ülle.

'I'm not Mama,' Regan replied, tugging the sweatshirt the rest of the way. Why had nobody on the discussion boards mentioned the Mama thing?

Before she tried putting the jeans on Ülle, she thought twice about it.

'You need to go again?' she asked, pointing at the toilet.

Ülle shook her head.

'You'll tell me when you have to?' Regan asked, and Ülle nodded. Regan wasn't sure she should trust her, but she dragged her to the living room anyhow. After sitting her on the couch, she got the jeans around her feet and worked them upward. Once they were past the knees, she helped Ülle to stand and lean against her, then hiked the jeans the rest of the way. Finally, Regan buttoned them and stepped back, holding Ülle by the elbows to keep her stable.

'Think you can stand on your own?' Regan asked.

Ülle nodded again.

When Regan let go, Ülle swayed but stayed upright. Beaming at her achievement, she took a step forward. Regan reached out to steady her, but Ülle waved her off.

'Okay, big shot,' said Regan. 'Go for it.'

Ülle took a second step, then a third, squinting in concentration. Regan readied herself to make a saving grab, but Ülle got all the way to the kitchen before her knees buckled. Regan caught her and eased her into the same chair as before.

Leaning into Ülle's nape, she inhaled. Still no buzz. The black spigot was barely an inch from her lips. She remembered the pleasure it had brought and grew ashamed, then angry with herself. The whole point of flatpacks was that you didn't need to feel any shame. They'd be with you, unconditionally, right until the end.

'Mama, what does I here?' asked Ülle.

Regan hesitated. She'd read that sometimes they asked such questions. You weren't allowed to tell them the real answer. According to the dealer's website, some people had done it, and there'd been 'adverse consequences.'

'Hmm,' said Regan, trying to remember the sentence you were supposed to tell them. 'I guess one answer is, you've been put here to comfort me.'

On the website, the words had seemed pretty half-baked. Coming out of her mouth, they didn't sound baked at all. The website had fronted a whole fairy tale to share, too, with four days of creation and a journey by night, but she wasn't going to tell her that crap if she could help it.

'What is "comfort"?' Ülle asked.

'It means, like, feeling good,' said Regan.

'How I does comfort you?'

'Oh,' said Regan. 'All sorts of ways.' Then, because that made her sound like a slimeball, she added, 'You're comforting me just by being here.'

Feeling her face heat up, she led Ülle back to the kitchen, seated her, and presented the food options again. Ülle reached for the orange and rolled it across the table. The rolling was good to see, because it meant she might have enough coordination now to feed herself. When Regan produced a knife to peel the orange for her, though, Ülle shrieked. She pulled the fruit close to her chest and refused to hand it over.

They weren't supposed to refuse you anything. Regan thought about saying that to Ülle, but it might sound weird, so she let her keep the orange while she spread almond butter on a rice cake. When she held it out, Ülle looked down at the orange, as if to reassure it, before setting it on the table to accept the offering.

She bit into the rice cake and made a face. Opening her mouth, she let what she'd bitten off fall to the table. Then she handed the cake back to Regan.

'It's good for you,' Regan insisted. 'It's rice. You know about rice?'

'Rice,' said Ülle, nodding. She glared at the rice cake. 'That is not rice.'

So she remembered rice. What else? You weren't supposed to ask them what they remembered. The website said it could upset them to realize that their past had been wiped clear.

'Maybe try the quinoa salad,' said Regan. 'It's low-fat.'

She got out a plate and a measuring cup, dispensed half a cup of the salad, and put the plate in front of Ülle, along with a fork.

'You know about forks?' she asked.

'Forks,' said Ülle, sounding rueful. 'Yes, yes.' She took the fork and dug into the salad, showing off a dexterousness that confirmed her deep acquaintance with forkery. The first load made it to her mouth without mishap or complaint, and all of a sudden she seemed like an ordinary adult, eating an ordinary meal, except that whenever she bit down on a cube of turnip, she reached into her mouth, extracted the cube, and set it on the table next to her plate.

Regan measured out another half-cup of the salad for herself and poured a glass of wine. The bottle was from her father's basement stash, some cheap Finger Lakes vintage with a brackish undertone and a hint of winter tires. She returned to the table with her glass and found herself wanting to ask questions that she couldn't. Where are you from? Did you have any family left? What was it like, becoming what you are now? She meant to alternate between one bite of salad and one mouthful of wine, but in her distractedness she ended up with an empty glass and a nearly untouched plate. By that point, Ülle was almost finished.

'How do you feel?' Regan said. 'Full?'

Ülle belched, and Regan could swear she saw a puff of green escape her lips.

'You want wine?' Regan asked. 'Like what I'm drinking?' Nobody had said you couldn't give them wine.

'Mama,' said Ülle with enthusiasm, so Regan looked in the cupboard for a glass that wouldn't break if dropped. She found a plastic mug at the back that her mother had brought home from her posting in Luxembourg. She'd said it had survived an IED detonating at close range on the Rue Notre Dame, and Regan hadn't asked for details. They didn't talk about that sort of thing.

Once Regan had poured some wine into the mug, Ülle took it and cautiously extended her tongue toward the liquid. After a taste, she began slurping it, longer each time. At one point, she tipped her head back to gargle before swallowing, then looked at Regan with a mischievous grin. Regan poured herself another glass and drank half of it in a single go.

When Ülle was done, she set down the mug and studied Regan's face.

'You is here alone?' she asked.

Regan felt her skin grow hot again. 'Thanks for pointing that out,' she said.

Ülle's gaze went around the kitchen. 'Where is we?' she asked.

The question reminded Regan of something that Ülle needed to be told.

'We're in my house,' Regan said. 'And we can't go outside. It's the most important rule, okay? Or bad stuff will happen. As long as we stay in here, everything will be fine.' She took another slug of wine, draining the glass.

'You no eat?' said Ülle when she'd finished. 'You is so skinny.'

'Why, thank you, Ülle. That's totally your business.' She gave Ülle the same look that she gave her parents and anyone else who made such remarks. Usually, the look was enough for the person to change the topic, but Ülle seemed not to notice.

'Anyhow, I'm fat,' Regan said. 'I haven't run for three months.'

'Mama,' said Ülle, sounding sympathetic or maybe bored. Her grassy scent had grown sweeter, headier. Regan drank it in and thought she might finally be starting to feel the buzz, except she'd onboarded so much wine that it was impossible to say which sensations came from what.

'Come on,' she said. 'Let's watch some garbage.' It wasn't how she'd imagined the night going, but it felt like the easiest thing to do.

Taking Ülle's hand, she led her to the living room. Ülle seemed unsteadier than before; she kept pulling in the wrong direction, and Regan had to reach for the wall to keep herself upside-up. Once she'd deposited Ülle on the couch, she returned to the kitchen and poured two more glasses of wine. Somehow she managed to spill both of them. She knew she was supposed to care, but a wire in her brain had come unsoldered.

They watched a sitcom that Regan had never heard of, about a crime-fighting family with everyday problems. By the end of it, she'd finished her glass of wine. Then, because Ülle hadn't touched hers, Regan finished that one, too. They sat through another episode of the same show, but Regan spent less time watching it than she did watching Ülle. Or not watching her, exactly – being aware of her. She imagined taking a photo of them sitting on the couch like this and sending it to Lucinda. What would Lucinda do?

Lucinda would do the same as anybody. She'd call the cops, they'd break down the door, and Regan's mother would come home and care about Regan's welfare for a few days, and everyone would agree that it had all been a cry for help. No way was Regan going to have that pinned on her.

By the time the episode finished, the sun had set and the room was dark but for the flickering light from the TV. Regan handed the remote to Ülle, who pressed random buttons. In the darkness, a pair of tiny white rectangles had eclipsed her pupils, and the silvery varnish on her skin seemed to glow. Her face was free of wrinkles now. She couldn't be more than twenty-five.

Regan felt the urge to touch her. Nothing gropey, just a fingertip on the soft polish of her jawline. She wanted to lean against Ülle's shoulder. It would be totally innocent. If Ülle objected, Regan would pull back. The dealer's website had been very explicit about consent. It seemed strange for the dealer to care, and Regan had almost taken it for a joke, except the website wasn't much of a laugh factory. Probably the dealer was trying to make their business seem less skeezy, less like the dark-web dirtbag operation it was, when they knew as well as anyone that nobody was going to stop you from doing whatever you wanted. A comment on one of the discussion boards had stayed with her, something from a troll or maybe just a dude being honest: '*Flatpacks be killing you, you should at least get to bang them.*' All the upvotes and downvotes had nearly cancelled each other out. Regan had downvoted it and sworn to be gallant.

Still pecking at the remote, Ülle managed to arrive at a documentary about the plague, of all things. Regan had seen the documentary before. The History Channel ran it pretty much on repeat, because humanity was a collective morbid freak. At that moment, the screen was showing a map of eastern Europe with arrows radiating outward. Then flocks of sheep bulldozed into pits. A dead dog with a crown of flies. After a few more shots, the bodies would be human.

'We don't want to watch this,' she said. Grabbing the remote from Ülle's hand, she poked the power button. Except the power button must have moved, because the TV wouldn't shut off. She tried again, and the voice of someone jabbering about closed borders got louder. She mashed her palm across as many buttons as she could, and finally the voice shut up and the picture changed to a settings menu.

Beside her, the light from the screen had turned Ülle's face indigo. She stared at Regan as if about to start making accusations. Dammit, the plague hadn't been Regan's fault. She hadn't been the one to come up with flatpacking. A whine started in her head and grew louder.

'Why are you looking at me like that?' she said. She began to feel dizzy, even though, as far as she could tell, she was only sitting on the couch.

'Mama,' said Ülle. When she placed her hands on Regan's face, Regan shivered.

Once, Regan's mother had liked to hold Regan's face in that way, although never with such gentleness. It had always been to inspect her, to make sure her face was clean or, during Regan's mascara phase, to ensure that her makeup hadn't smeared. Lately, when her mother had landed at home for any length of time, she'd been too preoccupied by the disaster zone that was Regan's father to keep up the inspections. Now Ülle was looking at her as her mother used to, with the same unstinting focus.

The air between them swam, hot and sodden. At some point, Ülle's meadowy smell had turned tart. There wasn't going to be any buzz to ease things, was there? No serenity and sense of wellness, only the shitshow presaged by Toodles in the bedroom. Regan's hair falling out in clumps. Her skin weltering. The website had made it clear that once you placed the order, there were no tradesies, no erasies. You couldn't even crack a window or crank the AC. She was stuck stewing in Ülle's juices.

At least there'd be Ülle to console her. She wouldn't be dying alone. Regan imagined the two of them lying on their backs upstairs beneath the hallway skylight, looking up at a lactic ribbon of stars, Ülle's hand and hers finding one another, their mouths meeting in a friendly, surprised, totally innocent kiss.

'Mama, I is frightened,' Ülle said. She leaned over until she lay on the couch with her head in Regan's lap.

Regan stroked her soft stubble of red hair. 'Don't be scared,' she said. 'It's all good.' This last phrase was one she used often on the phone with her mother. She had become well-practised in knee-jerk lies.

Ülle's skull in Regan's lap sat firm and heavy. The spigot on her neck pressed into Regan's thigh in a way that sent a flutter through her, then began to hurt, before settling into a point of discomfort she could tolerate.

The heat in the room grew. Sweat trickled down her back. The menu on the television screen offered a choice of inputs, while the remote sat at the other end of the couch. This wasn't how she'd imagined their first night together. There wouldn't be many more. She took a few long breaths to test her lungs. They still worked fine; she just felt tired. Her lids grew heavy, and she rested her fingers on Ülle's neck.

She woke to find the TV turned off and her headache returned. The living room still held its sour scent, but Ülle had vanished.

Regan checked the bathroom. Empty. In the kitchen, the dishes from dinner remained on the table. She was about to look upstairs when she saw that the door to the basement had been left ajar. In her hurry down the stairs, her stress fracture flared and made her take a hop, and she thought how funny it would be if, right then, she tripped and broke her neck.

The light in her mother's office was on. Ülle sat at the desk with her back to the door, staring at the computer monitor, a pea-soup haze around her. From the doorway, Regan cleared her throat, and Ülle swivelled to face her.

'What are you doing?' Regan asked.

'I doing computer,' said Ülle.

'I can see that. What are you looking at?'

Ülle hesitated. Flatpacks were supposed to answer you straightaway.

'Jari,' she said finally.

'Jari? What does that mean?'

Ülle's eyes widened. 'Don't know,' she said.

Regan nudged Ülle aside to check the screen. She'd only ever heard of flatpacks being able to take on menial tasks, but if they remembered how to talk, they might remember how to use computers, too.

It looked like Ülle had figured out the browser, at least. The history showed a string of random websites seeming to follow from a search for a single term. *Jari*. Regan searched for it herself. Seventy-seven million hits. Based on the results, it seemed that Ülle had started clicking through them from the first one.

'Who's Jari?' Regan said.

Ülle gave another shrug. She was getting better at them.

'Is he someone you remember?' said Regan.

Ülle shook her head.

'Do you remember anything else?' Regan asked.

Ülle seemed to ponder the question. 'You blows in me,' she said. 'I remember the blowing.'

Regan's headache ratcheted up another notch. She didn't want to talk about the blowing. 'What about before that?' she asked.

Ülle's eyes ran back and forth across the carpet. 'Nothing is in me!' she cried. With a look of panic, she turned to Regan. 'Mama, who is me?' Bright green tears began to stream down her cheeks.

Regan put a hand on her shoulder. 'I don't know,' she murmured.

Seventy-seven million hits. If the manufacturer had done its job, none of those results would offer clues. The government had demanded a full scrub for every flatpacked person before being shipped over. They said it would promote integration. More likely, they just hadn't wanted people turning into bleeding hearts about their flatpacks' histories. Well, maybe it had been the right move. What good would it do Ülle to know where she came from? Given what people like her had been through, whatever she found out wouldn't be all pie and fries.

'I don't want you looking at the computer, okay?' said Regan. 'It's not for you.'

Ülle seemed unmoved. 'Mama,' she said, as if out of reflex. Then she yawned and rubbed her eyes.

'How long have you been down here?' said Regan. 'Did you sleep at all?' She glanced at the monitor. Five-thirty in the morning. Her stomach had cramped with hunger, and her headache was a Jurassic stampede. 'Come on,' she said. 'Let's get you to bed.'

In her room, she pulled aside the quilt, and Ülle clambered onto the mattress. Through the curtains came a low, pinkish light hinting at dawn. It was too hot for the quilt, so Regan just tucked it up over Ülle's feet and told her to call out if she needed anything. Regan was feeling virtuous and her headache was ebbing, and she was almost to the hallway, thinking that maybe now she could manage some Special K, when Ülle spoke.

'Mama, stay.'

There was something beyond plaintiveness in her voice. Regan turned to take her in, lying there with her bright eyes and, beneath the sweatshirt and jeans, her metallic nakedness. No, Regan was just hearing what she wanted to hear. For God's sake, the woman called her Mama.

With a sigh, Regan stepped back toward the bed. 'I'll stay until you fall asleep.'

Feeling chivalrous, she got in beside Ülle and stared at the ceiling. If Ülle wanted something to happen, she'd have to make the move. Regan's life was a string of fuck-ups, but she'd at least managed to go eighteen years without doing anything pervy to another human being against their will.

As they lay there, the sunlight strengthened and turned orange. Neither she nor Ülle spoke or moved. Was Ülle still thinking about Jari? A boyfriend, maybe. Husband. Regan wasn't going to ask. She pulled out her phone.

'Let me show you some photos,' she said.

Ülle dipped her chin to see the screen.

'This is my parents and me in Ireland,' Regan said, 'visiting the village where Dad was born. This is Mom helping me with my Grade 5 science-fair project. This is us at Halloween. I was the Beast, Mom and Dad were Cogsworth and Lumière – '

'They are died,' said Ülle matter-of-factly.

Regan frowned. 'No, Mom's in New Zealand. Dad's in rehab.' Ülle looked at her blankly. 'It's like reform school for addicts.'

'You are aliving by yourself?' said Ülle.

'I'm eighteen,' Regan replied. 'It's allowed.'

She turned back to her phone and brought up a shot of Paul. He always looked drunk in photos, even though he didn't drink. Regan called it resting shitface.

'This is my ex,' she said. 'I could never get a word in.'

'He is nice,' said Ülle.

Regan rolled her eyes and flicked to a picture of Lucinda. 'This is my other ex,' she said. 'Lucinda. She dumped me last month.'

'Dumped?' said Ülle. 'What does this mean?'

Regan ignored her and swiped to another photo. Lucinda again. The next three were of her, too. Regan swiped more quickly. There were shots from cross-country races, shots of teammates now away on scholarships, and more photos of her parents, rare ones from the few times in the last couple of years when her mother had been home and her dad hadn't been high.

She'd made it through most of the album before she realized that Ülle had fallen asleep. Regan switched screens and tried googling *Jari* and *Ülle* together, first with the dots over Ülle's name, then without. Both ways, there were ninety thousand hits. She tried *Yari + Ulla*, then *Jari + Oola*. Nothing in the first results looked promising. She went to the sites where people were documenting who'd been flatpacked and found nothing there either.

On the government page, they still claimed to have destroyed every flatpack that had been shipped over from Europe, never mind that in the past few months, half a dozen had made the news by popping up. The government said they must have been stolen from the factory before production was shut down, then smuggled across the Atlantic.

Once more, Regan found herself wanting to text Lucinda. Lucinda was into flatpacks, not in a sicko way, but because of the humanitarian angle. She was the one who'd told Regan about the dealer, back when they were together.

'You shouldn't be showing people this stuff,' Regan had said, straining her neck to see the website on Lucinda's phone.

'Why not?' Lucinda had asked.

'Because some of us are prone to depression and bad impulse control.'

'Oh, sweetheart,' Lucinda had said. 'You're too smart to get involved with something like this.'

If Regan were to call her now, she wouldn't tell her about Ülle. She'd just ask whether she'd ever read about a flatpack keeping some of its memory. Imagine, she'd say, if one turned up at your door and remembered a guy's name. What would you do?

Except she wasn't allowed to say that. It was another of the dealer's rules: no telling anyone what was going on. You could phone people, but you couldn't breathe a word about flatpacks. The dealer's site promised that they'd be monitoring all calls, texts, social media. A bluff, maybe, but she wasn't going to test it.

She turned to Ülle's sleeping body. 'You're everybody in my life now,' she whispered. 'Do you know that?'

Eventually, the phone ran out of juice. When Regan got up to plug it in, she saw that the floor was dotted with dead insects: a sowbug curled into a pellet, a pair of millipedes, ants of assorted shapes and colours lying on their backs. They must have been in the walls and come out in their death throes.

The hallway was the same. Houseflies willy-nilly on the hard-wood. At the top of the stairs, a mouse lay stretched out stiff with its teeth bared.

She went to her parents' mirror and checked herself again. No marks or discoloration. The air was a verdant borealis, yet she seemed unaffected. Paul had once claimed that he was immune to poison ivy, that he could cha-cha in a patch of it without catching an itch. Could it be the same for her? None of the buzz, but none of the other effects either? Nobody on the discussion boards had mentioned such a possibility.

With rubber gloves and a trash bag, she went around picking up the dead creatures. Then, in the basement, she googled *flatpacks* and *immunity* and got a bunch of articles about executives avoiding prosecution after the program was shut down. She paired *flatpacks* with *resistance* and then *survival* and got sites about the plague. She tried *flatpacks* and *delayed reaction* and got bloggers blaming the government for its slow response to the first reports of off-gassing. She would have kept on, but by now her stomach was nickering, and the only way to shut it up would be to feed it.

When she returned to the kitchen, she heard a scratching from the mudroom. It was Toodles at the cat flap, wanting back inside. She went to the door and laid her hand on the latch before drawing away.

'I can't do it, I'm sorry!' she said. 'I love you, but I can't!'

The scratching persisted, and his meows were fingernails on her brain. Maybe letting him back in wouldn't be so bad. It would prevent a neighbour from finding him and bringing him over, growing suspicious when she didn't answer the door. But it wouldn't be fair to Toodles. He wouldn't know what he was getting into. And she couldn't handle him dying before she did.

In the kitchen, she measured out a cup of Special K and poured it into a bowl. She measured out half a cup of no-fat soy milk and poured it on the cereal. She counted out six raisins and set them on top. Then she devoured the whole thing so quickly that she felt even worse and needed to lie down.

When she got back to her room, Ülle was lying diagonally across the mattress, still asleep. Regan rolled her over to one side with the scent of swamped hayfield in her nostrils. She let her fingers graze Ülle's nape and wander upward until they reached the spigot behind the ear.

Regan couldn't help herself. She slid her body closer to Ülle's so that they were nearly spooning, then put her lips on the spigot, which still tasted of ChapStick, and blew. When Ülle didn't wake, Regan blew harder, propping herself on an elbow. Soon she felt the same sweet wallop between the temples as before. With a shudder, she withdrew and curled up, clutching a pillow. Eventually, her heartbeat slowed to an even pulse. The sun shone greenly through the room's haze, dim enough to let her fall into a doze.

When she woke, Ülle had vanished. She was in the basement again; Regan felt sure of it, and the thought enraged her.

Then she turned over and saw a silhouette in the door frame. It was Ülle. She had taken off her clothes, and she was grimacing and pressing the sides of her head with her hands.

'Mama,' she whimpered. 'Is hot. I feel bad.'

She tottered forward and crumpled to the floor. Regan scrambled out of bed.

'Head feel too big,' said Ülle. A bulge had formed on her forehead like a clot of air was trapped beneath the skin. 'Was you blowing into me?'

'I didn't know,' Regan pleaded. Nobody had said not to do it.

Another knob of skin swelled up, this time on Ülle's chin. Her silver gloss had dulled. It no longer seemed so perfect; there were salmony freckles along the arms, and beneath her belly button was a five-inch smile of scar.

She began to writhe on the carpet. 'Mama, help me!' she cried.

'What do I do?' Regan said. 'I don't know what to do!' If she dialled 911, they'd send the cops, and Ülle would be as good as dead anyhow.

Lucinda then. Lucinda could google things at her end, talk through solutions. Lucinda knew how to handle a crisis.

Regan grabbed her phone and brought up Lucinda's name. For an instant, her gut roiled. She'd promised to stop calling. Their conversations had got kind of pathetic. She called anyhow.

There was no answer. Lucinda had never bothered to set up voice mail, and Regan could think of nobody else to try. Well, that wasn't quite true. There was Paul. But she really didn't want to call him.

Ülle groaned, then shrieked. Regan dialled him. Again, no answer. The beep took ages to come.

'Hey, it's me,' she said. 'There's an emergency.'

She hung up and tried to think. Maybe it was like a snakebite and she could take out what she'd put in.

Lying crossways to Ülle, head to head, she inchwormed forward until her mouth was once more at the spigot. This time she sucked on it. The air she inhaled was caustic, like how she'd imagined piss would taste. Each gulp scorched her throat. As she worked, though, she could sense the tension in Ülle starting to ease, so she kept going. After a couple of minutes, she began to feel light-headed. Her lips grew sore, the spigot slimy. Finally, she stopped and flipped onto her back, panting, the surf of her breath crashing in her ears.

She glanced at Ülle's torso and saw that no more bubbles had formed.

'Mama,' said Ülle. It was a moan carrying a tonic of relief, and Regan understood that things might eventually be all right.

'Mama, thank you,' Ülle said. Her hand reached for Regan's. 'You make me better.'

'I'm not your mama,' said Regan. 'But I'm going to look after you.'

It was, if not an empty promise, then at least a time-limited one, but Regan didn't tell Ülle that. Instead, she tried to sort through what had happened.

'Where are your clothes?' she asked. 'Did you take them off because you were too hot?'

'I take them off before that,' Ülle replied. 'I give them to the man downstairs.'

The hairs on Regan's neck jumped, and the skin on her forearms puckered into goosebumps. 'What man downstairs?' she cried.

'Man from box,' said Ülle.

All the blood in Regan ran berserk. 'You're shitting me,' she said. A voice in her head said that she needed to stand, but she couldn't move. Then the force pinning her to the floor dissolved, and she got to her feet. A second later, she was running for downstairs, and with every step her stress fracture lit a Roman candle of pain to mark the way.

TWO
LETTER TO LITTLE ONE

Little one, in case we should ever be separated, let me tell you now about a man named Jari, who was among the last of a dubious family, and about a woman named Ülle, who loved him.

In their country across the ocean, Jari's family was known as Mormor's family. Even Ülle, growing up in her backwater village, had heard of Mormor's family. Ülle assumed that at some point in decades past, before Mormor took charge, there had been a Morfar along with her, heading up the clan, but Ülle never heard talk of him, not even after she began working for Jari at his home in the city. There, she cared for his three-year-old daughter much as I care for you, little one, with all the fears and hopes that follow on from being held responsible for another's life.

It was Jari's wife who hired Ülle. At the interview in the couple's high-ceilinged apartment with its many rooms, as the flaxen-haired girl played on the rug with her dolls, Ülle tried to stay upright, sitting at the edge of a couch with cushions so thick and yielding that they threatened to swallow her. In all innocence, she asked the wife what Jari did for a living, not yet knowing whose family she was dealing with, and the wife, who until that point had seemed gracious and easeful in her armchair, stiffened.

Have you heard of Mormor's family? she asked.

Ülle nodded, feeling herself go red.

Jari is Mormor's grandson, said the wife, her tone suggesting that this fact was the source of all her unhappiness. He keeps the family business out of the house, she continued. It wouldn't involve you.

Of course, Ülle replied.

The pay is generous, said the wife. And there are advantages to working for Mormor's family. You would be safe – as safe as someone can be at a time like this. But I must stress the need for discretion. The smallest breach of trust –

I understand, said Ülle.

In an ideal world, Ülle would have turned down a job working for such people, but the world was not ideal. She took the position, doted on the child, cooked and cleaned, hoarded her earnings, bore the suspicious looks from shopkeepers who heard her country accent, and tried never to meet the gaze of the dark-browed husband, Jari, who came and went on unnamed errands, while she marvelled at the fact that the wife had been so confident in her marriage as to employ a woman several years younger than herself.

It turned out that the wife's confidence was well-founded, little one, because over the next five months, Jari showed no interest in Ülle. He barely spoke a word to her until after his wife and child were dead of the worm.

Do you have someone? he asked Ülle then. She didn't tell him that she'd left her family to work for his, that she'd needed money to bring her parents and brother away from their village before the worm took them, that she hadn't saved enough in time. She told him only that her people were gone.

Then stay with me, he said.

She stayed with him. He was as sweet and tender as a broken man could be. His parents had died, too. His aunts and uncles. All his cousins, save three. Then two. He and Ülle loved each other while the worm rampaged and the country slid into ruin. Famine and lawlessness. Blackouts for days. Hospitals made charnel houses. Packs of feral dogs roaming the boulevards, howling in the night like devils.

Jari continued to go out every day on business, never speaking of his occupation beyond assuring Ülle that nine-tenths of the rumours about his family were lies, that he worked for Mormor at a factory, and that his grandmother would never ask him to undertake anything dishonourable. Ülle kept to the apartment, maintaining what busyness she could, now that she was cooking and cleaning just for two. A pair of tiny shoes with pink laces still sat by the door. Toys still filled the chest in the den. Ülle's own things stayed in her windowless room at the far end of the apartment, while she slept each night in the bed where Jari's wife had once lain beside him. Then, one afternoon, Ülle returned from the grocer's to discover that the wife's and daughter's things had vanished. Even the furniture in the girl's bedroom had been spirited away. When Jari came home from work, they didn't speak of what was missing, but she saw him register the absences with sunken eyes.

That he required so little of her made loving him feel safe. The daily separateness, the evenings of companionable silence. Ülle had no interest in assuming the role of nurturer or in any way dredging up her past life. Still, during the hours alone, she often ended up online, searching for news about people in her village. Only a handful seemed to remain. The posts by those now dead mostly followed the same pattern: news of a diagnosis, worsening symptoms, testaments of love and gratitude, misplaced expressions of hopes. Sometimes there were rants about God, the government, immigrants, traitorous friends and relatives. Occasionally there was a final post by a family member, but those were mostly for the early victims. Ülle herself had written such things for her parents and brother.

She never posted about her own circumstances. When she'd left the village, there'd been no running water and every plot in the cemetery had been filled. If she announced now that she enjoyed a life of city comfort, it would sound like gloating.

Life wasn't so comfortable, though. Ülle and Jari lived in fear of the worm. No, that's not right, little one; it wasn't fear, exactly. They lived in expectation. So many had died that it seemed certain the worm would take them, too. The smallest stomach pang was reason for panic. Every time Ülle ventured outside, she went with trepidation. The scientists on television insisted that the worm wasn't contagious, but who knew? Their claim that it had lain dormant for years in its victims could scarcely be believed. People wore surgical masks everywhere. Acquaintances greeted each other without touching. You washed your hands ten times a day. There was a test for the worm, but almost no one took it, because it cost so much and there was no cure anyway, only flatpacking, and flatpacking was even more expensive than the test. Almost nobody in Ülle's village could have afforded it.

She was sure that Mormor's family could afford it, but there'd been no flatpacking for Jari's wife and daughter, nor for anyone else in the clan. Ülle never asked why not; it wasn't her place. She'd found it hard, though, to keep herself from pleading for the daughter, for I must tell you, little one, that she'd come to love the girl.

Then, one night in bed, Jari confessed to her that the decision not to flatpack his wife and daughter had been Mormor's.

Mormor is a very religious woman, he said. She's of the conservative school.

In their country, ever since the discovery of flatpacking as a way to neutralize the worm, two schools of thought had arisen among those who feared God. The progressive one welcomed flatpacking as a way for the afflicted to avoid the temptation of suicide. The conservative school viewed flatpacking as itself a form of self-murder and, thus, a mortal sin.

Of course, Jari added, I'm also of the conservative school.

Ülle nodded. Until then, he'd never spoken of himself as a believer. Ülle herself considered flatpacking better than a drawn-out death from the worm, a view she had developed after witnessing the last hours of the wife and daughter, but she perceived that Jari didn't want to hear it. She was expected to be of the conservative school, too. Not because of him, but because of Mormor.

You're allowed to disagree with Mormor, he said, as if in answer to Ülle's thoughts. You can't argue with her, though. All her life, she has sacrificed herself for the family. Now there are so few of us left. One must be loyal.

He sounded like he was trying to convince himself.

Was your wife also of the conservative school? Ülle asked. As soon as she saw the pain on his face, she regretted saying it.

Yes, he replied. Yes, certainly, she was.

After that, he launched into a diatribe against flatpacking. He said that when you were flatpacked, it might kill the worm inside you, but you lost your memory, stopped being you. You were sent overseas to a country where you had no rights. They claimed to be taking you out of compassion, but they did it only because you came to them packaged all neat and tidy, your past squeezed out of you, nothing more than a pet.

Yes, it's terrible, said Ülle. Privately, she wondered how strong his wife's faith in God must have been for her to accept such a death for herself and her child.

Jari began to weep. Ülle rolled over and straddled him, nuzzling his cheek. She felt the scratch of day-old stubble as he whispered that he loved her.

He had first uttered these words three weeks to the day after his wife and daughter's funeral. It had been Ülle's first time in bed with him, and she had fought to conceal her bewilderment. He barely knew her. They were betraying the dead. But in the days that followed, when he kept saying the words, she said them back.

Let's have a baby, he said now.

A baby, she repeated. Until that point, he had insisted on taking precautions against a baby. She remembered how, her first time lying with him, she'd caught him staring at the horizontal scar below her belly button. He hadn't said anything.

Neither had she. He knew that her people were gone; she needed to tell him nothing else. Now, as she straddled him, she asked him what had changed.

My family is almost finished, he said. Mormor's family. I need to stop being so selfish.

You want to have a baby for Mormor? said Ülle.

No, he said. For us.

Ülle didn't know how to reply. She really believed that he was a good man.

All right, she said. For us.

From then on, little one, Jari abandoned his precautions when they did the thing that people do to make a child. They did it raging at the Fates. They did it dreading the worm. They did it with the ghosts of their dead looking on. They did it for pleasure and indifferent to pleasure. They did it with a sense that their lives had ended and that the two of them were the real ghosts.

Almost right away, Ülle put on weight. She knew it couldn't be due to a baby; she was just eating more. It was the opposite for Jari, who seemed suddenly to adopt the habits of his rail-thin wife. Too much butter, she had complained of Ülle's cooking, so Ülle had switched to oil. Too much oil, the wife had said, so Ülle had secretly switched back to butter. Now Jari pleaded a poor appetite and refused desserts, skipped meals. He said the smell of the city ravelled his stomach.

The more Ülle considered it, the more convinced she was that it would be wrong to raise a child in their country. They needed to find a way to the Americas. The border was closed, and nobody made it overseas except as a flatpack, but surely nothing was impossible if you were rich enough and knew which palms to grease. One night, Ülle asked Jari whether Mormor had ever spoken of emigration.

It's not that simple, he said. Our family has interests here.

For the first time, he confessed that his workplace was a flat-packing factory. The only one in the country. His family ran it for the government, a lucrative arrangement from which they couldn't just walk away.

How strange, Ülle thought, that Mormor opposed flatpacking yet ran a flatpacking factory. When Ülle asked Jari how this could be, he only shrugged.

After that conversation, she decided it would be best to leave the matter of Mormor and the Americas for a while. A week later, though, Jari returned from work at the end of an afternoon and announced that Mormor wanted to meet her.

I told her of our plans for a child, he explained.

Ülle was horrified.

Why would you tell her? she cried. If no child comes –

She felt certain that disappointing Mormor was one of the worst things you could do.

There will be a child, he insisted.

Little one, Jari didn't realize that, earlier the same day, Ülle's period had arrived. She'd been agonizing over how to break the news. Jari would know as well as she did that infertility, in men and women both, was a symptom of the worm.

When does Mormor want to meet? she said.

Tonight, he replied. We must leave right away.

Right now? she exclaimed. I can't. My clothes, my hair –

Mormor doesn't care about such things, he told her.

Give me a few minutes, at least, she said, then rushed to the bathroom. She was bent over the sink, scrubbing blood from her underwear, when he entered without knocking. Before she could hide it, he saw what she was doing.

It's all right, she said quickly. We'll keep trying.

He nodded, averting his eyes.

You mustn't say anything to Mormor, he told her.

Without further discussion, and without eating the dinner that Ülle had prepared, they got into Jari's sedan and took to the nearly empty streets. She resisted an urge to break the silence, not wanting to distract him, knowing that when driving in the city, you had to be on the lookout for ambushes, madmen with guns. Only once they reached the highway did either of them speak.

We're moving to the Americas, he said. Mormor has decided it.

It should have been welcome news, but something in his tone unnerved her.

Who is moving, exactly? she said.

It's still to be decided, he replied. That's why Mormor wants to talk with you.

I thought she wanted to talk about us having a child, said Ülle.

That, too, he replied. It's all bound up together. Listen, whatever you say to her, you mustn't lie. She'll know if you're lying.

I would never lie, Ülle said.

In Mormor's eyes, he went on, the most important thing is trust. If she decides that she can't trust you –

Ülle laid her hand on his and felt the tension in his fingers as they clutched the wheel.

It will be fine, she said.

She'll ask about your past, he said. About bad things you might have done. Things you thought nobody knew of. No matter what, speak truthfully.

Ülle thought about the bad things she'd done in her life, and her stomach knotted. As you go on, little one, I hope you'll be able to think of yourself as a good person, but nobody can think of themselves in that way when asked to reflect on their worst deeds. In such moments, you're sure that nobody would love you if they knew who you really are. The only way we're able to live with ourselves is by being allowed to forget what we've done.

Ülle thought of asking Jari whether Mormor had told him about the bad things Ülle had done, but she didn't want to hear the answer. Their relationship might survive his possession of such knowledge, but only if they never spoke of it.

What about my period? she asked. You said not to mention it.

He fell into a frownful silence.

Does anyone else know of it? he said. A doctor? A druggist?

Nobody, she replied, and he went quiet again.

I don't think Mormor will ask, he said finally. If she does, stick to the truth.

Hardly anyone gets pregnant right away, said Ülle. We just started trying.

Yes, he said. That's fine, say that.

Ülle had always assumed that Mormor lived close to Jari's apartment, but they drove along the highway until they were in the countryside, following increasingly decrepit roads through fields barren of crops and thick with crows. Almost an hour went by before they stopped at the entrance to a long lane barred by an iron gate. Beside it stood a gatehouse with no one in it. Jari got out and dragged the gate open.

The lane passed between witch elms with amputated branches. It led to a sandstone mansion with two wings stretching from a portico like a great bird in flight. The shrubs beneath the mullioned windows had gone wild from want of tending. The broad lawn was dotted with white shapes. When Ülle looked closely, she saw that they were mountain hares, at least two dozen of them, each as big as a terrier. It seemed strange for their fur to have already lost its colour when it was only the middle of October.

They've been here since I was a child, Jari said. They're white all year. There's a fence that keeps them in.

When he and Ülle exited the car, the hares didn't pause in their grazing. They only looked on in a manner that seemed smug and thuggish.

At the front door, Jari knocked, but nobody answered.

There should always be someone, he said.

The wind blew brisk and cold, carrying the smell of snow. Ülle drew up her collar. Finally, the door was opened by a squat man in a sealskin coat, his face slick with sweat. When he saw Jari, he straightened, seemingly embarrassed, and ushered them into a dark foyer.

The power's out again, he told Jari. No one has managed to start the generator.

Behind him, from somewhere deep in the mansion, came a long, flute-like scream.

Is that Panizov? said Jari, sounding more weary than alarmed.

He's in the last stages, the man replied. The worm will show itself soon.

Is Mormor with him? Jari asked.

The man shook his head.

She's in the cottage, he said, waiting for you and your woman.

The man glanced at Ülle, and she hastened to put on a smile, but he swung his gaze back to Jari without further acknowledgement.

While she's out there with her, the man said, you could try your luck with the generator.

Jari turned to study Ülle, as if appraising her readiness to meet Mormor. Within the mansion, the screaming started again.

I'll be fine, she told him. Go, take care of the generator.

The screaming persisted, and the man in the sealskin coat looked in its direction like a dog straining at its leash. Jari sighed and led her back out onto the doorstep. He pointed to the side of the mansion.

Follow the path, he said. The cottage is at the end. And remember what I told you. Only the truth.

After a brief kiss, he disappeared inside. The sun was slipping behind the horizon. The white hares seemed to have crept closer to the house. At this distance, they appeared dishevelled, their fur tufting like the hair of children just out of bed. Some were streaked with blood on their muzzles and haunches. Ülle shivered. She had lost her affection for hares one morning at the age of six when her father had handed her a knife and taught her how to dress one. A polite way of describing an impolite thing. She started around the house and down the path.

Everywhere she looked, the estate was in disrepair. The path lay rutted and potholed. The glassless frame of a greenhouse had been throttled by vines. On the far side of a slimy pond, a tall chain-link fence had been brought down by a fallen tree.

Ahead of her stood a house that she took to be the cottage. It had a slate roof with two gabled windows, and its walls were fieldstones, mustard and carmine, thickly mortared, as though with icing sugar. At the thought of Mormor waiting inside, Ülle felt her clothes grow hot and itchy. She had the feeling of being watched.

Glancing over her shoulder, she started. The hares had followed her. They were strung out along the path, loping with long legs that looked, in the way of all hares' legs, like the result of some demented surgery, stitched on from the bodies of a bigger species.

When she stopped in place, the hares stopped, too. She took in the blood streaking their sides, their twitching noses. They were only hares. There was no reason to be afraid.

They started to advance on her. Ülle shrieked and ran for the cottage. When she looked back, they were matching her pace.

Little one, I know that you'll laugh at this part of the story. You'll say that it's absurd for a grown woman to be terrified by a pack of hares. But I swear to you, if you'd been there, alone with those creatures behind you, you wouldn't have thought it funny.

Reaching the cottage door, Ülle knocked as hard as she dared, her fear of Mormor almost as strong as her fear of the hares. There was no response. She looked back to the animals, which had stopped a few paces away and waited, as if curious to see whether someone would answer.

From behind the cottage came a scurry of whiteness. Ülle yelped, taking it for another hare, but it was a sheet of paper, carried by the wind toward the hares in fits and starts. More sheets followed from the same direction, then scores of them, darting and tossing across the grass. As they reached the hares, the animals flattened their ears.

Rounding the cottage, Ülle saw that the pages were blowing from a place on the lawn where dozens of banker's boxes sat next to a firepit ringed by stones. Most of the boxes were stacked beside each other in a row, three high, like the beginnings of a wall, but a few lay tipped over, disgorging reams of paper.

She was drawing near to them when she heard a deep groan, as though from the boxes themselves. Stopping, she listened to the groan grow into a howl. Then a ridge of flesh surfaced behind the boxes, breaching like a whale's back. She watched as it rose to become a human figure, gaining its feet with a bawl of effort.

It was a woman, the biggest Ülle had ever seen, a head taller than her and twice as wide. She had a thick frizz of white hair, and she wore nothing but plain grey underwear and a grey undershirt. The fabric lay taut against her skin, looking ready to burst its seams. Whatever it didn't cover was muscles. Muscles of an impossible size. Her neck was thick as a stump. Her back spread like a wing suit. The lines in her calves were valleys plunging through cordilleras of rock. Her skin was a sickly yellow, pocked by acne scars across her limbs and torso. Veins that looked filled with the blue ink of ballpoint pens snaked along her every inch. She lurched and shook, grunting and soughing, fighting to stay upright.

Ülle wanted to run. She would sooner face the hares than this person.

Then the woman turned in her direction. Her face was swollen like it had been made of dough with too much yeast. Her eyes were yellow and rolled up into her head. A jaundiced foam rimmed her lips, which had drawn back in a rictus.

The woman's eyes rolled back into view and fell upon Ülle. She felt the gleam of a cold intelligence weighing her. Then the woman's limbs began to jerk stiffly, as if some unseen force were compelling her to move and she were resisting with all her might. Scattered about her on the grass were a pair of workboots, a heap of black fabric that might have been a dress, and a canvas satchel noosed by a thick strap. She started toward the satchel, eyes bulging with the strain. After a few lock-legged steps, she stumbled and fell, collapsing on her back with a bellow. Ülle was about to go to her when she heard the woman's voice.

Neeeed, she said. Neee-eeed.

For all the effort that speaking the words seemed to require, they carried a note of stolid expectation. From it, Ülle knew three things. She knew the satchel contained something that would save the woman. She knew she was being called on to administer it. And she knew the woman was Mormor. But then, she'd known that from the start.

Little one, what will you think of Ülle if I tell you she hesitated? It seemed obvious that she couldn't delay for long. For all she knew, Mormor could die. Yet no sooner had Ülle thought as much than she began to consider the consequences. Without his grandmother, Jari might stop burying his wishes beneath hers. Without her, he might take Ülle with him to the Americas.

Mormor's chest began to rise and sink with ominous speed. Ülle looked back toward the mansion. There was nobody coming. She went for the satchel and dumped its contents on the ground.

A ring of keys. A silver-plated pistol. A leather pouch with a zipper down its side. She opened the pouch to find a plump vial half-filled with pink fluid, as well as a syringe tipped by a needle in a plastic sheath. That was what Mormor had been saying. Not *need*, but *needle*.

Then Ülle noticed a second vial in the pouch, identical to the first but with purple fluid instead of pink. Examining the vials together, she saw no writing on them. They were missing the same amount of liquid. Ülle held them both for Mormor to see.

Are these what you need? she asked. An injection?

Mormor gave a nod.

Which one? said Ülle. Pink or purple?

Mormor's gaze flitted from one vial to the other, her mouth still caught in its rictus. Ülle watched her lips slowly purse.

Puh – , Mormor said. Puh-puh.

Purple? said Ülle. How much? A whole syringe?

Hah, said Mormor.

Half, said Ülle. All right then.

Removing the sheath from the needle, she jabbed the needle through the vial's rubber cap and drew out the purple fluid until it filled half the syringe's cylinder.

Where do I stick it? she said.

Mormor tried to speak, but there was only a rattle in her throat. Scanning her body, Ülle saw that her skin was spangled with little marks on her neck, her shoulders, her arms and legs. Dozens of dots like mosquito bites, along with bruises of varying sizes and shades, from butterscotch to raisin black. It seemed that it didn't matter where the needle went. Ülle selected the meatiest portion of Mormor's thigh and stabbed it in.

A yellow foam hissed out around the point where the needle was sunk. Ülle depressed the plunger, then withdrew the needle. Air shushed from the puncture, strong enough to snuff a candle. A bit of the foam caught her knuckle and began to sting. Even once she wiped it off, her skin still burned.

It seemed impossible that the shot would take effect so quickly, but in seconds Mormor's breathing grew more regular. The yellow drained from her face, and although it might have been a trick of the light, Ülle thought she could see her skin settling and shrivelling, her features becoming those of an old woman. Still lying on her back, she shook out her limbs and stretched her neck, rocking her head from side to side.

Ülle glanced toward the mansion, hoping to spot Jari. A stand of birches by the pond was pale and ghostly in the dusk. The wind had died, and the few stray sheets of paper that remained in view lingered where they lay, caught in ruts or nestled by the cottage wall.

Then she saw the hares. A dozen of them only a few steps off, watching.

Shoo, she cried, gaining her feet. Get away! She ran at them, waving her arms, braver now that she was responsible for another person's welfare. The hares hopped lazily out of her path.

Leave them, said Mormor. They're harmless.

Ülle turned to watch her raise herself into a sitting position. They were chasing me, Ülle said.

It's because I feed them, said Mormor.

There's blood on their fur, said Ülle.

They fight each other, said Mormor.

She tried to stand and fell back. Ülle went to help her up, but Mormor waved her off.

A little thing like you, said Mormor with a laugh, and Ülle didn't know whether Mormor was referring to the preposterousness of Ülle lifting her or to the fact that Ülle had possibly just saved her life.

Mormor tried again to stand, this time with success. She stumbled to the place where her boots and clothing lay and pulled the black dress over her head. It was plain and shapeless. When she tried to slip on the boots, they didn't seem to fit her.

Feet are still swollen, she murmured. She gathered the boots in one hand and pointed toward the cottage. Come, she said.

They walked across the grass, scattering the hares, Mormor's gait so heavy that Ülle could swear the ground trembled. When they reached the cottage, Mormor stepped inside and flipped a switch. Nothing happened.

Power's still out, she said. Wait here.

She disappeared into the building. A minute later, she returned with a jerry can in one hand and a cigarette lighter in the other. Returning to the firepit, she doused the boxes there with gasoline, working as though she'd done this sort of thing many times. Then she set the boxes alight and stepped away just in time to avoid a whoosh of flame. Soon the fire reached above their heads and a funnel of sparks helixed into the near-night. Standing beside her, Ülle felt her skin tauten from the heat, while the flames made Mormor's face seem to regain its yellow pallor.

It was at this moment, Ülle thought, that the interrogation would begin. The moment at which she'd have to prove herself a suitable mate for one of this woman's last surviving grandchildren.

Mormor said nothing. The silence became unbearable. Finally, from sheer nervousness, Ülle spoke.

What would the pink vial have done? she asked.

Once out of her mouth, the question sounded impertinent, but Mormor seemed untroubled.

The pink vial? she said. Oh, it would have killed me.

Ülle gasped, and Mormor tutted.

It's nothing, she said. An everyday problem. Did Jari not tell you?

Ülle shook her head.

It's these muscles, said Mormor, looking down at herself. She began to flex them, running through her biceps, triceps, shoulders, and calves, turning each momentarily into a perfect specimen of strength.

The doctors gave them to me, she said. At your age, I was an athlete. Now, if I don't use them, they become unstable, so I have to take the pink stuff as a stimulant. The purple is for when they're worked too much. Not much call for the purple nowadays.

She waved her hand toward the wall of boxes, barely discernible beyond the bubble of firelight.

Don't tell Jari what happened, she said. He doesn't like me lifting things.

I won't say anything, Ülle replied.

I wanted to finish before he got here, Mormor said. I must have passed out. You have to do everything yourself these days.

Mormor stared into the fire, looking wistful.

I used to have a grandson named Snaut, she said. He kept track of my levels for me. Tested them three times a day. He liked to joke about it. He'd say, *What other man has drawn Mormor's blood and lived to tell of it?*

She gave a chuckle, then grew sombre.

He was a good boy, she said. Before he died, he told me I had so much acid in my veins, the worm would never have a chance with me. He said, *Your muscles are keeping you alive, Mormor.*

Her eyes flashed in the firelight. She turned to Ülle.

What about you? she said. Why are you still living?

What do you mean? said Ülle, startled.

Everyone has a story they tell themselves, said Mormor, to explain why the worm hasn't taken them.

I don't have a story, Ülle replied. For me, it's just luck.

Not because you're a good girl? said Mormor with a smile. Because you've led a virtuous life?

Ülle felt Mormor's eyes slide over her as if she were a stick of furniture being sized up for purchase.

I know things about you, Mormor said. The life you've led.

This was the moment about which Jari had warned Ülle, the one for which she'd been steeling herself. Still, the words twisted her guts.

She imagined asking how dare Mormor judge her? Mormor, who lived in a mansion, who never in her life would have worried whether there'd be money enough for food. But an outburst like that would get Ülle no closer to the Americas.

Does Jari know, too? was all she said.

Mormor shook her head.

You have to understand, said Ülle. The worm had reached my village. I was on my own in the city –

I don't need to hear it, said Mormor. I know the things one must do to survive.

She turned back to the fire.

Have you heard of the Cravitzes? she said. The Bortolotti gang? Ülle said she hadn't.

That's because a long time ago I made hard choices, said Mormor. To survive. To keep my family safe.

You did what you had to do, said Ülle. As she spoke the words, her attention was only partly with Mormor. Her mind had been cast back to her first weeks in the city, before Jari's wife had hired her. Homeless, hungry. Times she would be happy to forget.

Mormor walked over to the boxes beyond the pit. Grabbing one in each hand, she carried them back and tossed them on the fire like they were nothing.

All that matters is my family's future, she said. That's what I care about. Jari has told you we're emigrating?

Ülle nodded.

It will be difficult, said Mormor. We'll take only what's necessary.

Ülle wondered if she was being called upon to plead the case for her own usefulness.

Jari wants a baby, said Mormor. This, for him, is the important thing.

If Mormor were someone else, Ülle would have asked her whether it was really Jari for whom a baby was so important.

I've told him that if he wants a baby, there are plenty of women in the Americas, Mormor continued. But he says you're the one to have it. What do you think of that?

Before Ülle could answer, there was a burst of blinding illumination. Floodlights from the cottage springing to life. The glare made the lawn seem harsh and tawdry. The grass was too green, the shadows jagged. The hares had disappeared from sight.

Ülle looked toward the mansion and saw Jari walking down the path. As he reached them, Ülle expected him to embrace her, but he only stood at her side with an expression of concern.

Mormor, did you move all these boxes? he said.

All these boxes, said Mormor mockingly. You think I can't outlift you five times over?

You're not wearing a coat, he said. It's freezing.

Enough foolishness, she replied. Come, I want to speak to you.

As the three of them crossed the lawn, he reached for Ülle's hand. Then, when she went to follow Mormor into the cottage, he tugged her to a standstill.

Can you wait out here? he said. From his tone, she could tell she'd be breaking a taboo if she accompanied them inside. But she didn't want to be stuck out there in the cold and the dark with the hares lurking someplace nearby.

I'll wait in the house, she said.

You can't, he replied. Everyone there is occupied.

The car then, she said, expecting him to object. Instead, he fished the keys from his pocket and handed them to her.

We won't be long, he said. With that, he stepped into the cottage and closed the door.

In the car, she pulled her jacket tight around herself. She didn't want to start the engine and be accused of wasting gas. She didn't want to turn on the radio, run down the battery, and strand them there. She listened to the wind rustle the trees and watched a strip of cloud sift the moon. Time stretched long past the point when Jari and Mormor should have finished an ordinary conversation. Ülle felt certain that if they were still talking, it was because everything was being decided, that her fate hinged on the words passing between grandmother and grandson. At this thought, she screamed, knowing that nobody would hear her and nobody would check on her if they did. She wasn't family. She didn't want to be. Her survival might depend on making it to the Americas, but the only thing she desired was to be back in Jari's apartment, lying in her bed in that windowless room that had been the first and only room in the world she'd been able to claim as entirely her own. If she closed her eyes, she could almost imagine she was there.

She fell asleep like that. When she awoke, Jari was sitting beside her, and the car was moving through the night, the lights of the city drawing near.

He told her of his meeting with Mormor. How he'd insisted that he wouldn't emigrate unless Ülle came with them. How

Mormor had threatened to disinherit him, how he'd refused to back down, and how, finally, she'd reached into a drawer and produced travel papers for the three of them. The whole ordeal had been a test of his commitment to Ülle.

The only thing that matters to Mormor is that you and I do our duty, he said.

You mean a child, Ülle replied, and he nodded.

Little one, Ülle herself could not have told you why exactly she said what she said next. Perhaps vanity demanded that she assert her role in Mormor's relenting. Perhaps Ülle needed to confess something to Jari in compensation for other things she wasn't admitting. Or perhaps there's simply a part of us that refuses happiness, both our own and other people's – a part of us that, feeling happiness's approach, actively seeks to repel it.

Whatever the reason, she found herself saying that he mustn't breathe a word to Mormor, but that Ülle had quite possibly saved her life.

As she explained what had transpired, the story came out clean and easy: the hares and the boxes, the hulking crepuscular shape, and the choice of pink or purple vials. She finished by repeating Mormor's adjuration not to speak of what had happened. It was only then that she turned to him and registered his look of horror.

Why did you tell me that? he exclaimed. She told you not to say anything.

What does it matter? she replied. How will she ever know?

As soon as she asked the question, the answer came to her with alarming certainty. Jari would tell her. If not that night on the phone, then the next day, or the next time he visited the mansion.

He seemed to guess her thoughts.

I won't tell, he said. But you shouldn't have put me in this position. Don't you see? This is just what she fears. A stranger disrupting the family.

Am I a stranger to you? Ülle cried.

You are to Mormor, he said.

Am I not part of your family? she persisted.

He didn't reply.

They reached the city and drove back to his apartment. Once there, she didn't slink back to her room and lie down alone as she wanted, knowing it would cause offence. But the thought of entering his bedroom and doing with him the thing that people do to make babies was more than she could bear. As they prepared for sleep, she got ready to remind him of her period.

In the end, no reminder was necessary. Lying down next to her, he kissed her on the cheek and turned away.

Little one, this action was hardly different from what Ülle herself would have done if she hadn't been a poor, orphaned peasant and Jari the scion of a family with the power to save her life. Yet the fact that he did it, and with such apparent ease, outraged her. She thought then of telling him the greatest secret of their relationship, even though it might bring the relationship to ruin.

The secret was that, for the past few weeks, while he had stopped taking precautions against a baby, Ülle had not. Cached in her room was a blister pack of pills, and she swallowed one of them each morning.

Little one, I can already hear your protestations. Why would Ülle risk being discovered? How long did she think she could keep up the deception? What of the fact that the longer she went without conceiving, the more Jari would suspect that one of them had the worm, and the greater the chance that Mormor would demand she be cast off?

Little one, Ülle herself could not have answered these questions.

That night wasn't the first that she thought of telling Jari her secret. Every time previous, she'd balked, and every time, the reason, more than anything else, had been the bald fact of her life having too much disorder for her to add more. That night, the same fact stayed her tongue again.

Ülle sensed that he hadn't yet fallen asleep. She wanted to say something that might let them start the next day on a better footing. Her mind spun through the events at Mormor's estate.

How is Panizov? she said finally. Given what she'd heard in the mansion, there was only one possible answer, but she thought that Jari might appreciate her asking.

Panizov? he said. Panizov is dead.

That's awful, she replied. I'm sorry. How long did he work for your family?

Work for us? said Jari, sounding surprised. Panizov was my cousin.

A tide of regret bore through her.

I – I didn't realize, she said. You never mentioned him.

No, I suppose not, he replied. We weren't that close. There used to be so many of us.

THREE

HELPMATE

When Regan reached the living room, the box in which Ülle had arrived was lying on the floor with both ends open. Except it wasn't the same box, because the first one still sat where Regan had left it. A pair of scissors lay spread-eagled beside the second box, and near the couch was another sheath of plastic, crumpled and empty, sliced apart in half a dozen places.

Over by the coffee table, a man was stretched out on his back, clothed in the sweatshirt and jeans in which Regan had dressed Ülle. His head and feet were almost two-dimensional. He had the same red hair as Ülle's, along with Neanderthal eyebrows and a black pencil moustache. Acne scars pitted his cheeks, too deep for the silvery varnish on his skin to obscure. The jeans covered only the tops of his deflated calves, while the sweatshirt sleeves didn't reach his flatbread wrists.

'He comes when you asleeping,' Ülle said from the top of the stairs. 'I open him.' She descended, a little stiff-necked but otherwise moving well. The bulges on her face had subsided to welts. She still wore no clothes. 'He is Jari, I think,' she said.

Regan looked again at the man, his nub of Adam's apple, his pocked face, and realized his moustache was fake. Somebody had drawn it in magic marker. Who would have done something like that? A worker at the factory, maybe, with too much time on their hands.

'How did he get here?' Regan asked. She didn't bother to keep the suspicion from her voice.

'In box,' said Ülle. 'The door makes bing-bong. I find him there.'

Regan glanced at the front door and saw that her seal of tape had been broken. 'Did you have him sent here?' she said. 'Did you order him on the computer?'

Ülle shook her head, but Regan didn't believe her.

'He can't stay,' Regan said. 'You know that, right?'

'I not want him,' muttered Ülle. Then her face took on an expression of surprise, as if she were shocked by her own bitterness.

A burbling erupted from the man, and a tremor ran through him, bringing him slightly closer to human girth, like he was a microwave popcorn bag and the first kernel had exploded.

'You need to blow in him,' said Ülle. 'I not do it strong enough.' To demonstrate, she exhaled tepidly.

Regan didn't want to blow into him. 'Let's get some clothes on you first,' she said.

Leading Ülle upstairs, Regan dressed her in another set of her mother's things. Then she took her to the basement and checked the computer. Unless Ülle knew how to clear the browser history, nobody had visited the dealer's website since Regan had made her purchase.

'Who is he?' Regan demanded. 'Your boyfriend? Husband?'

'I do not know,' Ülle whispered.

'You know his name is Jari,' Regan pointed out.

Ülle seemed unhappy to be reminded. 'Maybe is not his name,' she said. 'Maybe I am wrong.'

'Then why do you think that's what he's called?'

Ülle knitted her brow. 'Is in me,' she said after a time.

'Just the name?' Regan asked. 'That's all you remember?'

Ülle looked stricken and didn't answer.

Regan went to the dealer's website in search of a return policy. There wasn't one, not even contact information. Maybe this was how they operated: if a customer didn't die after the first flatpack, they sent another to finish the job. They might have a lackey out there right now, watching to see how things wrapped up. Regan could demand that he take back his delivery. It had only been a day, though; why would they send another flatpack so soon? Maybe the guy had been meant for someone else but Regan's address had popped up in the deliveryman's system. She could stick the flatpack back in his box and set him on the front step. It would be breaking the rule against unsealing the house, but it was unsealed now anyhow. If some flunky was keeping a lookout, he might realize there'd been a mistake and deliver the box to whichever suicidal ideator had actually ordered it. Maybe the dealer had already detected the slip-up and was trying to contact her.

'Let's go upstairs,' she said, rising.

'Yes,' said Ülle. 'You blow into Jari. Maybe he tells you how he gets here.'

In the living room, Jari lay with eyes closed and limbs limp, yipping quietly like a dog dreaming. Regan went to the window and peeked between the drapes. No vehicle in the driveway or cul-de-sac. Nobody in sight. But if they were spying on her, they'd probably be hidden. She could try opening the door and calling out, but the next-door neighbour's Bronco was in the driveway and she didn't want to make a scene.

Jari gave another groan.

'You blow in him now,' Ülle insisted. 'Is hurting him to be halfway.'

Regan didn't want to know that. 'You shouldn't have blown into him in the first place,' she said.

She had an urge to just leave. If she took Ülle with her in her father's car, stepped on the gas from the moment they exited the garage, and drove for a few miles *Mario Kart*–style, they might be able to escape, even if somebody was waiting to chase them down. After that, what next? Sneaking Ülle into a motel room and feeding her takeout? Maybe they could find a cave in the woods, or they could stay in the car and keep moving.

In her mind, they'd got almost to Yosemite when there was a knock at the door. The deliveryman, it had to be. She went and peeped through the hole.

It was Paul, close up and peeping back at her.

'Regan?' he said. 'Regan, I can see you in there.'

She'd forgotten that she'd called him. Maybe, if she stayed still, she could wait him out. As long as Ülle didn't come over and wreck things, he might think his eyes had played a trick on him.

Ülle came over and wrecked things. 'Your ex?' she asked. At least she had the sense to say it quietly.

'Don't move,' Regan murmured. 'Maybe he'll go away.'

'If you don't let me in, I'm calling the cops,' he said, then knocked more loudly. She could hear her phone ringing in her room.

'Don't let him in,' she whispered to Ülle before heading upstairs.

The phone went silent just as she got there. Picking it up, she saw that he'd been calling and texting like a psycho for the last ten minutes. She jabbed at his name and took a deep breath.

'Go home,' she said when he answered. 'Everything's fine.'

'Open the door, will you?' he said.

'I was cooking and set off the smoke alarm. I've taken care of it now.'

'So why won't you let me in?'

'Because there's a situation,' she replied. 'We've got bedbugs.' It was the excuse that the dealer's website had recommended. 'The fumigators said no visitors.'

'They let you stay in there?'

'I'm wearing a mask,' she said. 'Sorry I called. I panicked. I don't need any help.'

'Come outside and talk with me, at least.'

'I can't. I'm crawling with bedbugs.'

She heard him sigh.

'You said it was an emergency,' he reminded her. 'What am I supposed to think? What if I go home and something happens?'

'Like what?'

'I don't know. Something.' She knew he wouldn't say what they were both remembering. 'I'm not leaving until we talk face to face.'

'Fine. Go to the living room window.'

'I can't. There are bushes.'

'Just, like, step into them.'

Downstairs, she motioned for Ülle to help her, and together they dragged Jari into the dining room. Through the phone, she could hear Paul swearing at the bushes.

'Are you at the window yet?' she asked. Returning to the living room, she pulled back the drapes just enough to show herself. He was standing on the other side in his work uniform.

'Where's your mask?' said his voice through the phone, just after his mouth formed the words.

'I took it off,' she said. 'You think I'm going to let you see my super-cool fumigation mask?' Then she retreated behind the drapes. 'Show's over. Go home, okay?'

'That's not what I meant by face to face,' he said.

He swore his way out of the bushes, and then he was knocking on the door again.

'Leave me alone, will you?' she cried.

'In ten seconds, I'm calling the police.'

'To arrest the bedbugs? Why won't you just trust me? I told you, I can't open the door.'

'Why not?'

'Please, Paul. Please? We're talking life-or-death here.'

Immediately, she knew it had been the wrong thing to say.

'First it's a false alarm, now it's life-or-death?' he said. 'I swear, I'm calling the cops.'

'Don't you dare,' she said. 'If you hang up on me, I promise, you'll never see me again.'

It occurred to her that the dealer could be listening in on the conversation. But if they were, they'd know the dilemma she was in. They should understand what she was about to propose.

'Go to the back of the house,' she said. 'I'll meet you by the mudroom door.' At least the two of them wouldn't be such a spectacle there.

In the mudroom, she ripped the tape from around the door and stepped outside. Making a visor of her hand, she peered toward the ravine at the back of the yard, looking for the glint of binoculars or a charging goon. She could hear the twitchy whisking of the neighbours' sprinkler. The warm sun and the breeze on her face reminded her what a dankness the house had become. She yearned to see Toodles lounging on the grass, but he was nowhere in sight.

When Paul came around the corner, he no longer looked angry, only concerned. It would have been better if he were still pissed off. She hated it when he started talking as though her welfare were the most important thing in his life. His voice went half an octave higher, all mushy singsong, like she was a human tantrum to be soothed, while his eyes turned moony, showing the world that he was capable of such big feelings, such boundless empathy, because he loved her oh so much and her situation was so amazingly pathetic.

'Is it your dad in there?' he asked. 'Is he having another episode?'

'Keep your voice down.' She hated it when he brought up her father. Also, when he said *episode*. 'He isn't here. He's still in rehab.'

'So what's going on? Don't tell me smoke and bedbugs.' He glanced at the mudroom door. 'Is Lucinda with you? Is she messing you around again?'

'Give me a break. I haven't seen her for weeks.' Regan's resentment of the fact must have sounded as obvious to him as it did to her, because he scowled.

'Well, good,' he said. 'She wasn't right for you.'

'Because she's a girl, you mean,' said Regan. She couldn't help it; she knew about all the bullshit that got preached at his church.

'No, I told you before. It's about complementarity.'

'Like, *Hey, Regan, nice ass.* Yeah, I could have done with more of that.'

He didn't laugh. 'You know what I mean,' he said. 'I wish you'd take me seriously for once.'

Regan bit her lip. Paul took everything seriously. Taking track seriously had made him captain of their team, and taking his job seriously had got him elected the union steward at work – the youngest in Tkaronto, he liked to brag. In a few months, he'd be moving to Cornell and taking his studies seriously. Last year, when he'd started taking Regan seriously, she'd felt flattered and a little overwhelmed. He'd made it seem as if there was something in her, not him, causing such passionate devotion. For a while, it had felt nice.

Over the six weeks they'd been together, he'd acted like it was his sole duty in life to compensate for everyone else letting her down. He'd heaped scorn on her therapist. He'd called Lucinda a selfish, immature trust-fund kid, even though, at that point, she and Regan had only ever been friends, and Regan thought she'd done a pretty good job of not giving him any obvious reason to feel jealous. He'd shaken his head every time she told him about her parents, too, and he'd sworn to be there whenever she needed him. Each morning at school, he'd slipped a Post-it into her locker. Sometimes it had featured a motivational quote or a declaration of his love, sometimes just a clumsy hand-drawn heart with one ventricle a little flabbier than the other. One night at his house, alone in his bedroom while he tried to convince his parents that he and Regan needed the door closed to focus on their homework, she'd looked in the wastebasket and found a bunch of balled-up Post-its that all had the same heart, drawn over and over, lumpish first efforts at the ones he'd left in her locker. It had made him sweeter in her eyes, but it hadn't made her love him.

'You wanted to see me face to face,' she told him now. 'Mission accomplished. So you can skedaddle, right?'

'You should come back to the store,' he said. 'People have been asking about you.'

'Like who? Probably the same ones who thought I was just slumming it there.'

'There's a strike vote next week. We'll need you.'

'No, really, I'm done there.'

He stared at her for a time.

'Are you off the meds again?' he said.

She hated when he asked about her meds. 'It's none of your business.'

'Sorry. It's just that they made a difference – '

'We're not talking about this.'

He crossed his arms over his chest. 'If I leave now, who's going to look out for you? Are your aunts and uncles checking in?'

He knew all those people were overseas. She'd never even gone to visit them. Her mother said that she didn't feel a connection to anybody over there, that there was no obligation. She never seemed to realize that Regan might actually want to go.

'Paul, nobody in my family gives a damn,' Regan said.

It was the wrong thing to say, not because it was untrue, but because it wasn't going to get him off the property.

'I give a damn,' he said. 'You know that, don't you?'

She did, but she wished that he'd stop demanding that she admit it.

'I've been thinking,' he said. 'You've been so down about the scholarship thing. But you don't need a full ride from track. You could do Grade 12 again and get an academic scholarship. You know as well as I do, the only reason you didn't ace the SATs was because of things that came up.' It was another of his favourite euphemisms: *things*. 'You just need to – ' He stopped himself.

'I need to what?' she said. 'I always love hearing what I need to do.' She wanted to tell him that there were two flatpacks in her house and she needed to get back to dying. She wanted to say that when she'd sat down at that desk to write the SATs, it had been forty-eight hours since she'd last eaten.

'Forget it,' he said. She could tell from his face that he was giving up. He talked a good game, but in the end, he was like everyone else. Well, it wasn't his fault. She was too much for anyone to handle.

He stepped forward to hug her. His hands fluttered past her ribs and came to rest on her back, his fingers on the knobs of her spine, taking stock, weighing her by touch. It was an old habit for him. The first time he'd seen her naked, it had taken him a moment to find something nice to say. Then it had been six weeks of him silently calorie-counting her plate every time they ate together, while he put away food like it was nothing, even though he ran half the miles she did.

'I appreciate you coming by,' she told him. It was the last time she'd see him, and she wanted him to remember her in a good way. 'I hope the vote goes how you want it.'

He said thanks. Then his gaze shot back to the house. 'You sure there's nobody in there?' he said. 'I heard something.'

She turned toward the mudroom door, worried that she'd see Ülle opening it, but it was still closed. 'Just an old house making noise,' she said.

As gently as she could, she told him he should go. His gaze remained on the door. With a silent prayer, she went and opened it. There was nobody. She stepped inside before turning to wave.

'See you later,' she said.

'Okay,' he said. 'I'll call you.'

'Sure. Just don't freak out if I don't answer. You need to give me some space.' She forced a smile, then closed the door and locked it.

The murk inside the house seemed to have grown thicker. The air felt algal, like a fish tank left uncleaned. She took a deep breath and felt no chafe in her throat, no heaviness in her lungs. When she arrived in the dining room, Jari still lay uninflated on the floor, while Ülle was standing where Regan had left her. But her eyes were round as teacups.

'A man!' she whispered. 'There was a man!'

'Just my ex,' said Regan. 'He's gone now.'

'Not him!' said Ülle. 'A man with mask!'

The words jolted through Regan. 'Where?' she said.

With a look of terror, Ülle pointed, not toward the door but behind Regan.

In the middle of the dining room table sat a piece of paper. It had a scrawled arrow pointing in Jari's direction, along with two words in thick, red ink.

HE STAYS.

A cold sweat gathered on Regan's neck.

'Is the man still in the house?' she asked, and Ülle shook her head.

'He says if you go out again, next time you are not so lucky.'

Regan felt like throwing up. At the living room window, she peeked out and saw Paul getting onto his mountain bike. She drew away from the glass and waited a minute. When she looked again, the cul-de-sac was empty.

Except no, it wasn't.

Three doors down, a beige van sat in the driveway. It pulled out and slowly circled the cul-de-sac. The driver was in shadow, but out of the darkness came a ghoulish smile, full of shark's teeth, and a wagging index finger.

The van drove off at a crawl. She prayed not to see the flash of brake lights. When it came, she swore. The van turned into a driveway, reversed, started back toward her. It was a few yards from the cul-de-sac when it pulled to the curb. From this distance, the reflection on the windshield was too strong for her to see the driver's face.

Five minutes passed without any further movement. She closed the drapes and returned to the dining room, where Ülle sat cross-legged on the floor with Jari's head in her lap. His face had puffed out further, and his magic-marker moustache had grown gaps in it, so that it resembled a line of Morse code.

'Did the man hurt you?' Regan asked Ülle.

She said that he hadn't.

'Did he just write the note and leave?'

Ülle nodded, but it felt like she was holding something back.

'What else did he say?' Regan asked.

'He asks how I feel. He asks if I feel pain.' Then she added, 'He gives Jari a kick.'

'He kicked him? Why?'

Ülle shook her head in bafflement.

'What kind of mask was he wearing? Could you make out what he looked like?'

Ülle reflected. 'Big man,' she said. 'Big neck.'

'He didn't say anything else? He didn't do anything?'

Jari began to whimper where he lay.

'You must blow in him,' said Ülle. 'The hurting is bad.'

Regan didn't want to blow in him. She still couldn't believe that Ülle hadn't played a part in bringing him there. Even if she hadn't, blowing into him would mean more things to worry about. Better to stick him in the basement as he was.

Then she imagined him down there, unable to move, his whimpers coming up through the floorboards.

She returned to the living room and checked on the van. It was gone. That should have made her feel better, but it had the opposite effect. If she was going to be creeped on, she wanted to know where the creeper was.

'Fine,' she announced. 'I'll blow into him.'

In the dining room, with Ülle looking on, she knelt and put her mouth around the spigot on Jari's neck. It tasted of hand sanitizer. How did she even know the taste of hand sanitizer? It was probably better that she couldn't remember. After wiping the spigot with her shirt, she started over, hoping that she might at least experience again the pulse of good feeling she'd got from blowing into Ülle. But it never came.

'We should get him out of these clothes,' she said when she'd finished. 'If we wait until he's puffed up more, we'll have to cut them off.' He looked about the right size for her father's stuff to fit.

As she went to stand up, a wave of dizziness sent her back to her knees. Jitterbugs of light squiggled through her field of vision.

'You need eating,' said Ülle. 'Lie there. I bring you food.'

Regan was used to skipping breakfast, but she didn't have the wherewithal to argue, so she lay on the floor beside Jari while Ülle went to the kitchen. She came back with a glass of apple juice.

'I don't drink juice,' said Regan. 'Too much sugar. It's just for baking.'

'You give it to me yesterday,' Ülle pointed out.

'That's different,' said Regan.

'How different? You drink the wine, no? Is sugar, too.'

Alcohol had its own set of rules, but Regan didn't feel like explaining them, so she took the glass and sipped. She managed half of it before the acid sweetness became too much.

Ülle went back to the kitchen, returning with a plate of quinoa salad and a fork. 'Half a cup, yes?' she said. 'Low-fat.' Her voice was full of disdain. She set the plate on the table and disappeared into the kitchen once more.

Regan got to her feet and looked at the food. There was no way she could eat it, not after Ülle had made fun of it like that. She went to the living room and turned on the television. Out of the corner of her eye, she saw Ülle walk into the dining room with something in her hand and kneel beside Jari. Regan didn't want to watch her feeding him. Only when a commercial came on did she sneak a look. Ülle was using a paper towel to wipe his mouth. Her other hand held a glass of soy milk. Except Regan had used up the last of the milk for the Special K.

'That isn't milk,' she said. 'It's cream.'

Ülle gave a shrug. 'He likes it.'

Regan went to the window again. Still no van. From the kitchen, she checked the backyard. Nobody. Her cache of wine bottles sat on the counter. She uncorked one and took it to the couch, not bothering with a glass. Ülle gave her a look of disapproval.

'It's got sugar,' said Regan. 'Like you said.'

By the time she'd finished the bottle, Ülle had changed Jari into a button-down shirt and chinos and was coaxing him to take his first steps. Eventually, Ülle declared that he needed the bathroom. Regan didn't bother to ask how she could tell. When the two of them returned from it, Regan heard Jari call Ülle 'Mama.'

'I am not Mama,' Ülle said, sounding aggrieved.

'You tell him,' said Regan. Her voice seemed to register with Jari in a way it hadn't before, because he turned to her wearing a goofy grin and toddled in her direction.

'Papa!' he shouted. 'Papa! Papa!'

'Oh, come on,' said Regan.

Not long after that, she passed out. It was dark when her stomach woke her. She ran to the bathroom and threw up, then stayed huddled over the toilet, shaking. At some point, she felt Ülle's hand on her back.

'Papa?' said Jari from the door, full of worry.

'He is stupid,' murmured Ülle. 'All he says is *Mama, Papa*.'

'You swear you didn't bring him here?' said Regan.

'I am not lying,' replied Ülle stubbornly.

'But you know him from before. You were together.'

'Maybe,' said Ülle. 'I cannot remember.'

Whatever the truth was, Ülle seemed to be happy enough looking after him now. She must feel some kind of connection. Regan's stomach churned at the thought, and she stayed kneeling while he whimpered from the doorway.

'Regan,' said Ülle after a time. 'Why do you bring me to this place?'

Regan's gut convulsed again. All at once, she wanted to be off the cold tile. She lowered the toilet seat and sat on it. 'I told you before,' she said.

'You want the comfort,' said Ülle.

'I don't know what I wanted.'

It wasn't true; she did know. She'd wanted someone to talk to about why life had become impossible. Someone who wouldn't give her the bullshit she got from Paul and her parents and her therapist and her doctor and her coach and her fake friends on the track team. She'd wanted a warm hand on her forehead at the end. And maybe, before that, if they were both into it, a bit of sex. Well, she didn't feel like any of that now. She just felt sick.

'Your parents are not coming home?' said Ülle.

'Jesus,' said Regan. 'Stop it, will you?' She began to weep.

It was too much for Jari. He came in and began to pat the top of Regan's head.

'Papa!' he cried. 'Papa, Papa!'

'Cut it out,' said Regan. 'You're patting too hard.'

'You see how he is stupid?' said Ülle. She pushed him back, then stood between him and Regan.

'He might not stay that way,' Regan said. 'At first, you were the same. You just said *Mama*.'

They went to the living room and settled on the couch, Ülle once more positioning herself between Regan and Jari. Regan channel-surfed until settling on an old black-and-white movie with Jimmy Stewart and a nurse, but her stomach growled too much for her to concentrate.

At some point, Ülle nudged her, and Regan saw that Jari had fallen asleep. They agreed to leave him there. Regan brought down the comforter from her parents' room, and when she laid it over him, he blinked at her with his goofy smile, tongue lolling like he still wasn't in control of it, before closing his eyes again.

'I am tired, too,' said Ülle. 'We go to bed, yes?'

It was probably an innocent suggestion, but Regan still felt herself flush.

In the upstairs bathroom, she stripped to examine herself and found nothing except cellulite, then put on her pyjamas and went to her room. The lights were off. Ülle already lay in bed, under the quilt. Regan got in beside her and felt her palms grow damp. Her stomach wouldn't stop growling. If she'd been on her own, she could have ignored it.

'I'm sorry,' she said. 'I still don't feel good.' She went to the kitchen and ate the rest of the quinoa salad without even measuring. When she returned upstairs, Ülle didn't stir.

It was dark when Regan awoke to a snuffling from someplace in the room. Ülle lay beside her, unmoving. Regan got up and found Jari curled at the foot of the bed, blanketless, asleep, one of his legs twitching to the rhythms of a dream. She thought of waking him and insisting he go downstairs, but in the end she just returned to bed.

He woke her again some hours later, standing over her in the daylight, pawing at her side.

'Papa!' he said. 'Baby, Papa!'

Ülle appeared in the doorway to call him off, and he trotted over to her.

'He is very bad,' she said to Regan. 'I tell him not to wake you. When you are ready, come. There is something happens.'

'What is it?' said Regan. But Ülle departed without answering, and Jari followed her downstairs.

Regan found them in the dining room, standing near a crumple of plastic sheathing. On the table was another opened cardboard box, this time barely bigger than a toaster oven. Then she spotted what was on the table behind it. Lying on its back was the silvery body of a flattened baby boy.

Jari hopped in place and pointed at it. 'Baby!' he said. 'Papa, baby!'

She couldn't believe it. 'It's a joke, right?' she said. 'They're messing with us?'

Jari kept on hopping and shouting until Ülle told him to shush, at which point he went to the corner and wrapped his arms around himself.

'There were laws, for Christ's sake,' said Regan. 'It had to be voluntary. You can't get consent from a baby.'

What were they going to do with him? They didn't have anything for the kid to eat.

'You shouldn't have opened him up,' Regan said.

'Is not me,' said Ülle. 'Jari does it when we are sleeping.'

The parents must have arranged for the flatpacking, trying to save the kid from the plague. Regan took in his downy tonsure of red hair, his stubby fingers and toes squished flat like the ends of popsicle sticks. The spigot on his neck looked way too big. He couldn't be more than six months old.

Then Regan remembered the scar on Ülle's belly. She was still thinking about it when Ülle interrupted.

'This is good for you, no?' she said. 'This way, you die more quickly.'

It took Regan a moment to register the implication. The contempt in Ülle's voice.

'Three of us is more poison than two,' Ülle went on, glowering. 'Now you die like you want.'

'Who told you I wanted to die?' Regan said.

Ülle leaned across the table, picked up the box, and handed it to her. 'Look at it,' she said. 'You see, is okay that Jari opens it. There is no choice.'

Regan turned the box around and saw the words written on its side in magic marker: *THE BABY STAYS. BLOW IN HIM. KEEP YOUR LOVED ONES SAFE.*

The fuckers. Making threats, not even telling her what was going on.

'You must blow,' said Ülle.

'Okay, I get it,' Regan snapped.

'You should tell me things before,' Ülle went on. There was a hardness in her expression, as if she thought Regan deserved all that was happening.

'What things?' said Regan. 'Were you on the computer again?'

Ülle didn't answer.

'You want to know everything?' Regan said. 'First, tell me what's going on.' She pointed to the baby. 'You and Jari are its parents, aren't you?'

All at once, the anger in Ülle's face was replaced by pained confusion. 'I do not know,' she said quietly. 'It looks like him.'

'It looks like both of you.'

Ülle took in the baby, and Regan studied her expression, hoping for some hint of her thoughts or feelings.

'Nothing's coming back to you?' Regan asked.

In the corner, Jari had grown preoccupied by scratching his armpit. Ülle went over to grab his hand.

'You hurt the skin that way,' she told him.

Regan looked back to the baby and felt queasy. The way things were going, another box would turn up tomorrow, then another, and more after that, until there was a flatpack for every room and the green air scalded the walls, yet none of the arrivals would have the least effect on her. She'd just keep blowing into each one's neck before some goon was finally sent to kill her the old-fashioned way.

With a sigh, she bent to her task. The spigot on the baby's neck smelled of burnt coffee and tasted like balsamic vinegar. She blew out softly, counting ten between each breath, not wanting to rush the job and burst the kid wide open. Ülle sat in a chair and watched, while Jari lay at her feet and rubbed his head against her shins.

It took half an hour of gentle puffing before the baby began to approach a proper shape. Then he started to cry, and Regan lifted him off the table.

He was so light. Were all babies that way? She'd never held one. There was a time when she'd hoped for a sister, but years ago she'd decided that it wouldn't be fair to subject someone to the fate of having herself as a sibling.

Holding the baby didn't stop his crying. She gave him a few taps on the back, which had no effect either. He was probably hungry, and for that she had no solution.

'There's no milk,' she told Ülle. 'We're not allowed outside the house, and – '

'I know the rules,' said Ülle. 'I read them on the computer. Here, let me have him.' Without warning, she pulled off her sweatshirt.

'Whoa, hold on,' said Regan. But Ülle held out her arms, and Regan passed the baby to her.

Ülle brought the baby to her chest. Regan assumed that some kind of sacred scene would follow, with a halo forming over Ülle's head and bluebirds stunt-flying around her. Instead, the baby wouldn't latch on. When he finally did, it occurred to Regan that Ülle's milk might be tainted by the off-gassing. It was just a thought; nobody on the discussion boards had talked about the possibility. But then, nobody had mentioned lactating women being flatpacked. Regan searched on her phone and found nothing reliable, only some porno stories that were clearly made up, along with a few tales of miraculous flatpack births that had been downvoted so many times they couldn't possibly be true. A search for *flatpacked family* produced articles about couples who had gone through the process together, but none of the pairs resembled Ülle and Jari, and there was nothing about babies.

Ülle pulled the kid away from her chest and handed him back to Regan. 'Is no good,' she said, retrieving her sweatshirt. 'No milk. We must order it from the store. Maybe the man in the van does not see when it comes.'

Was Regan imagining it, or was Ülle's English improving? She was getting low-key pushy, too.

'We can't order milk,' Regan said. 'They could be tapping my phone and watching online.'

'Why do they give us baby if we cannot feed it?' Ülle said.

'I don't know.' She guessed that they didn't care much about the baby, but to say so would be to enter touchy territory. 'Maybe they figured we had milk in the house.'

'Maybe they figure we all die soon anyway,' said Ülle.

Regan's face went hot. She fumbled for something to say, an apology, a line of self-defence.

'The life for a flatpacked person after you open him is seven days, yes?' said Ülle. She gave a tight-lipped smile. 'Too bad you do not tell Jari this. Maybe he would not open the baby.'

Jari sat up and peered at them expectantly.

'I didn't know the baby was coming,' said Regan. 'Jari wouldn't have understood anyhow.'

'You do not tell me either,' said Ülle. 'You think I cannot understand?'

'It wasn't supposed to be like this,' Regan said. 'It was supposed to be just the two of us.'

'I read what they write on computer,' said Ülle. 'People like me and Jari are only pets.'

Regan's lungs felt suddenly short of oxygen. 'It's not like that,' she said. 'Everyone in your country was dying. Flatpacking was to keep you alive. You agreed to it.'

'The plague,' said Ülle sourly. 'I read all this.'

'They didn't know you were going to turn out – ' Regan hesitated. She'd been about to say *toxic*.

Ülle waved her hand dismissively. 'Yes, yes. We are illegal, we poison the air, we are stolen from factory. You buy me so you can die and do the sex with me.'

'I didn't,' Regan exclaimed.

'What, you did not buy me? You did not want to die?'

Regan couldn't bring herself to answer.

'Or is only the sex you did not want?' Ülle said. Then she turned her attention to the baby, who was rooting for her breast. 'I know they ask you not to tell me anything. Is bad, these people who help a young girl kill herself. Strange that you are not sick yet, no?' She reached down to pat Jari, who had fallen asleep at her feet. The baby began to cry again, and she gave it her fingertip to suck.

'Is better for Jari, not knowing what we are,' she said. 'It only makes him sad. Especially when he is the one to open the baby.'

'I won't say anything,' Regan promised.

'You still wish to die?' Ülle asked.

Regan's head began to hurt. She didn't want to talk about it, but she owed Ülle something.

'You have to understand,' she said. 'The plague mutated. It mucked up the chemistry in how they flatpack people. That's what started the newer flatpacks off-gassing and dying after a week. It turned out that they die eventually even when they're not opened, too. Like how a can of soup has an expiry date, right? That means inflating flatpacks can be good. That way, they get time out in the world.'

Such had been the reasoning of some folks online, at least. It was also what she'd told herself.

'So we are here from a kindness,' said Ülle. 'Not because you wish to kill yourself.'

The pain in Regan's head was growing. 'It's complicated,' she said.

'Is not complicated,' said Ülle. 'I do not wish to die. I do not wish Jari or the baby to die. I do not wish you to die.'

It wasn't fair, how easily the words made Regan weep. 'I'm sorry,' she said, wiping her face. 'I don't know what to do. We're trapped. If we go out, the dealer or the cops will get us. They kill flatpacks.'

Ülle stared at the floor for a time before looking up. 'We stay here and think of what to do,' she said. 'First, we find a way to feed the baby. Maybe he eats the cream, yes?'

Regan nodded and went to the fridge. There were only a couple of inches left in the carton. She warmed the stuff on the stove before bringing it in a glass to Ülle, who dipped in a finger and offered it to the baby. Tasting it, he scowled and squirmed. Ülle waited for him to calm down, then tried again.

'Maybe there's a way to make formula,' Regan said.

Once she'd found a recipe online, she went to the kitchen and plugged in the food processor. She cubed tofu, chopped a banana, splashed in some olive oil, pureed the whole thing, and scooped out a spoonful to taste. It wasn't terrible. With a bowl of it and a clean dishrag, she returned to the dining room. The baby was crying again, and Ülle was rocking him.

'Try this,' Regan said. After giving Ülle the bowl and dishrag, she drew up a chair beside them.

'You do it,' said Ülle. 'He does not like me.' Before Regan could protest, Ülle lowered the baby into her lap.

Once he had quieted a little, Regan dipped the end of the dishrag in the puree and offered it to him. He pushed it away. She tried again and got the tip into his mouth. Reflexively, his lips closed around it. A second later, his mouth started guppying. When he'd finished, the rag was clean. She drenched it again and watched him go to work. It was disconcerting, how happy she felt, just seeing him do that.

'Give him back,' said Ülle, reaching. 'I do it now.'

Regan didn't want to let him go, but he had Ülle's eyes.

Once Ülle was holding him again, he started to cry. When she offered him the tip of the rag and he didn't take it, she bounced him on her knee in a way that seemed a tad too vigorous, like the problem was a loose connection needing to be jostled into place.

'I can do it if you want,' said Regan.

'Is fine, no problem,' Ülle replied.

He was still mid-meltdown when Regan's phone buzzed. A text from Paul. '*Just checking in.*' In other words: *Reply or I'll call the cops.* He'd called them once when they were dating. She hadn't been serious about what she'd said, but she'd spooked him. A squad car turned up at her house, and the two officers wanted to know where her parents were. She told them the truth: her dad had fucked off somewhere and her mother was on the other side of the world. When the cops heard that, they didn't care that she was eighteen. They weren't satisfied until they had her mother on the phone and she'd insisted to them that no, Regan had never tried to kill herself, she was just a drama queen. Once they left, her mother called back and swore she'd come home unless Regan saw the doctor. Regan almost called her bluff, but the thought of her mother travelling all that way after telling everyone at the consulate about her looney-tunes child was too humiliating. The next day, Regan booked the appointment. Then she broke up with Paul. Funny, he should have been the one dumping her. Why would anybody stay with someone who said the kinds of things she'd said?

Now she wanted to warn him about the dealer's threat, but there was no way to do it. If she even hinted that things were unsafe, he'd call the police, and that would be it for Ülle and Jari and the baby. So she texted him: '*Thanks. Feeling okay. Need space.*'

Beside her, the baby had finished eating, and he gazed at Ülle with a doped-up look.

'Soon he will do the toilet,' Ülle observed.

Regan got to her feet obligingly. In the kitchen, she pulled out a dishtowel, then searched for safety pins. The air was hot and stale. The walls had an emerald shimmer. She wanted to turn on the extractor fan in the stove hood, but it wasn't permitted. The neighbours' dog was barking its head off, as it loved to do, and there was no chance of her going out and telling it to shut up. Not that she'd ever done that, but the idea that she could had always been a consolation.

There weren't any safety pins in the kitchen. Finally, she found some in her mother's office. Ülle didn't look impressed by them or by the dishtowel, but she handed the baby to Regan, laid the towel on the table, and origamied it into a triangle. Then she took the baby and set his silvery butt on it before folding the triangle up around him and pinning it like someone who'd done the job many times.

The baby didn't appreciate being on the table; he went back to crying. The noise woke Jari, who rolled over on the floor and put his hands against his belly.

'Hungry, Papa,' he said.

'Sure,' Regan replied. She went to the kitchen, with him following. 'What are you in the mood for?'

He sat at the breakfast table and stared at her. 'Hungry,' he repeated.

'Peanut butter sandwich it is,' she said.

She was thinking about how Jari would last longer than Ülle. In a few days, Ülle would stop off-gassing and keel over, and Regan would be left with him and the baby, making formula and sandwiches and cleaning green turds out of ad hoc diapers. A day later, Jari would go, and it would be just her and the kid for another day or two. Unless more of them had turned up by then. Or unless whatever kept them from affecting Regan kept them from dying, too.

As she got out the bread, something on the floor caught her eye. The cat's bowl. It was empty.

She turned to Jari. 'Did you eat the cat's food?'

He gave her his goofy smile. 'Kitty cat!' he said. 'Nice kitty cat!'

A pit opened in her stomach. 'Where is the kitty cat?' she said.

Jari kept grinning at her. She made to leave the room and motioned for him to follow.

'Show me where it is,' she said.

Jari's smile drooped. He didn't budge. 'Hungry,' he said.

'For God's sake.' She slathered peanut butter on the bread, slapped the slices together, and dropped them on the table in front of him. Then she went to the mudroom. The latch on the cat flap had been undone. She returned to the kitchen and snatched the sandwich out of Jari's hands.

'Did you let the cat in?' she demanded.

'Kuhhy cuh,' he said through a mouthful of sandwich.

'You did, didn't you?' She was shouting now.

Jari nodded with a blissful smile.

She found Toodles in her parents' room. He lay stretched out on the floor as he liked to be when having his belly rubbed. But he was half raw skin, half ragged fur, his jade eyes vacant, his mouth a frozen meow. She nudged the stiff body with her foot. Then she picked him up and carried him downstairs.

'He's dead,' she cried, squeezing him to her chest, feeling his coldness. He'd always slept on her bed. He'd let her cuddle him. She had no one else. When she tried to draw a breath, she couldn't. Everything inside her was gone. 'He's dead, and I'm not even sick.'

Ülle seemed unbothered by the news, but then, her first experience of Toodles had been him scratching her.

'Did you see Jari open the flap?' Regan said. 'Did you let him do it?'

'Jari is not understanding what he does,' said Ülle. 'He is too stupid.'

'You should have been watching him,' said Regan. 'You should have stopped him.'

When she was a kid, her mother had told her about the life-spans of small animals, and Regan had come to the awful real-ization that Toodles was going to die before she did. For a time, she'd played out fantasies of his final days. She'd made him a little deathbed and set him in it. She'd assessed the backyard, trying to decide where to bury him. In the end, she'd settled on the corner with the locust tree. Now she couldn't even take him there.

In the kitchen, she held him before Jari, resisting the urge to mash him into Jari's face.

'Look,' she said. 'Look what you did to the kitty cat.'

Jari's eyebrows rose in horror. He got up and ran for the dining room. 'Mama!' he shouted. 'Mama!'

Regan took a bedsheet from the linen closet, swaddled Toodles in it, and set him at the mudroom door, as close to his burial place as she could manage. She stayed with him for a long time.

Then she took the aspirin bottle from the medicine cabinet and the whisky bottle from her father's stash and carried them to the exercise room in the basement, where she settled herself on one of the rubber mats. Her father had installed a full-length mirror on the wall, thinking she would appreciate it. Long ago, she'd covered most of it with charts to record her training. From the mat, she could see only her bottom half. The pudging stomach, spindly calves. Feet that were too big for her body.

Aspirin had been her backup plan. She knew it wasn't pretty. A lot of barfing. Well, she could deal with that. How many times had she thrown up at the end of track workouts? The first day she'd done it, the coach had been impressed. She'd managed it a few more times before he lost his enthusiasm.

The first slug of whisky was disgusting. She made herself take another drink. Then she shook out half a dozen pills from the aspirin bottle, popped them in her mouth, and washed them down.

Once she'd done it, that was all she needed to know. She could end things if she wanted. Being alive was something she could keep up if it was a choice, not something she was stuck with. But God, the choosing wore on her. She'd been choosing for so long now, and each time, the memory of all the other times made the decision even harder. She wanted someone else to do the choosing for her for a while. She wanted to lie down and stop waking up as herself.

Before she could decide what to do next, Ülle appeared in the doorway. For some reason, she wore a raincoat belonging to Regan's mother, along with a pair of tortoiseshell sunglasses that Regan's father had given her mother as a birthday present.

'Baby does not stop crying,' she announced. 'The formula is shit. I go for milk.'

'You can't go out, I told you.' The idea of being stuck on her own with the kid made Regan suddenly aware of his absence. 'Did you just leave him upstairs?'

'No, Jari looks after him,' Ülle said. As if anticipating Regan's objection, she added, 'Is okay, I give Jari training.'

Then something seemed to catch her eye. Taking off the sunglasses, she looked past Regan to the place where the whisky and aspirin sat.

'I had a headache,' said Regan, hurrying to stand. 'Listen, you really can't leave the house.'

'I wait for night. Go through backyard.'

'Didn't you read what it says on the dealer's website? If they catch you, we're all dead.'

'He could be my baby,' said Ülle. 'Maybe it is me who lets them do it to him.'

The desolation in her voice was too much.

'If you let them, it would have been to save him,' Regan said. 'Nobody who had the plague survived.'

Instead of replying, Ülle went to the mirrored wall and perused the charts. Her looking made Regan feel suddenly exposed. The sheets recorded every repetition of every exercise she'd done in the past three years. In that time, she'd missed eight days. Paul and everyone else on the track team logged their training on their phones, but Regan preferred paper. For a minute or two each day, ticking boxes and filling in squares made life feel almost manageable.

'This is all from you?' said Ülle. 'You are very strong. Maybe it is what makes you still alive.'

She went over to pick up the aspirin. Holding it before her, she engaged it in a silent colloquy before closing her fingers around the bottle and giving it two quick, reproving shakes.

'I also have headache,' she declared. She deposited the bottle in the raincoat's pocket, then went to Regan and pulled her into a hug.

'I'm okay, really,' said Regan. 'I'm fine.'

Ülle didn't let go.

Regan remembered a time the previous summer when she'd been held like that by Lucinda, the two of them in their bathing suits on the dock at the cabin owned by Lucinda's parents. Lucinda was an inveterate hugger. She gave hugs so tight they made you cough. The embrace at the cottage had been after they swam to the point and back. Lucinda hadn't wanted to go, saying it was too far without an escort boat, so Regan had said fine, she'd do it alone. In the end, they swam out together, Regan beset by self-loathing, Lucinda lagging a few yards behind, though she was the stronger swimmer. In the last stretch on the way back, she came up beside Regan and, without a word, they began to race. Through the thrash and spray, Regan could just make out Lucinda in her peripheral vision, all churning legs and plunging arms. Lucinda had never tried out for the track team. She was shorter than Regan and weighed more. When she ran, she looked like she resented locomotion. In water, she was a machine.

The days at the cabin had been the highlight of Regan's summer. They'd let her forget the track season's disappointments and the fact that her father had bolted for a week in Las Vegas with his druggie friends. The roads around the lake were gravel, easy on her Achilles tendons. The last morning, Lucinda had promised that they could come back as often as Regan liked.

Regan pulled away from Ülle, her brain sparking with an idea.

'We're going to leave here for good,' she said. 'All of us, as soon as we can.'

'How?' said Ülle, sounding doubtful.

'My dad's car,' Regan replied. 'We'll wait until the van's gone. There's this cabin up north. My ex's parents own it, but they're out of the country.'

They'd have to break a window to get in. Or she could invent some ruse and ask Lucinda for the key. Hell, she could tell her the truth. As soon as she imagined it, telling her was what she wanted. But what if the dealer had bugged the phone? Better to stop at Lucinda's on the way.

'It is safer here, no?' said Ülle.

'I don't think so,' Regan said. 'They might keep sending flat-packs, or the dealer could come in here and murder us.'

'Why does it matter?' Ülle asked. 'You said that flatpack people die after seven days.'

'I could be wrong, though,' Regan said. 'I mean, I should be nearly dead by now, and I feel fine.'

Ülle seemed to think it over. 'You can call police,' she said. 'They will protect you.'

'The police would kill all three of you,' said Regan. 'You know how they get rid of flatpacks? They zip them up in a bag and let them suffocate.'

Ülle looked unfazed. Maybe she didn't know what *suffocate* meant.

'We should leave,' said Regan. 'And we should do it before there are too many of you to fit in the car.'

Ülle returned to the mirrored wall and examined the charts again. What had Regan been thinking, leaving them up for anyone to see? A meticulous record of wasted effort. She was sick of working out in a windowless basement. Sick of endless stretching routines and exercises for injuries that never healed. Sick of being in this house. Before Ülle could say anything, Regan went over and ripped the charts off the wall.

Ülle didn't try to stop her; she only watched until the sheets lay strewn across the floor and the whole mirror was exposed.

'All right,' said Ülle. 'We go to the cabin.'

Upstairs, they found Jari playing peek-a-boo with the baby. Regan went to the front window and saw the beige van parked at the other end of the cul-de-sac.

'I'll pack up,' she said to Ülle. 'If the van leaves, tell me.'

She thought about what to take. Clothes. Hats to disguise Ülle and Jari. For food, they could stop at a supermarket north of the city. They shouldn't need anything else. But what if they found the cabin occupied? Best to pack camping equipment, just in case.

Jari followed her to the basement. The camping gear, unused since her childhood, was piled in her father's recording studio. A tent, sleeping bags, her great-grandfather's wineskin, a kerosene lantern. A flashlight with batteries that weren't quite dead. When she turned it on, Jari yelped, then stamped at the yolky circle it projected onto the floor. She handed the flashlight to him and he took it upstairs, chasing the beam along the way.

She had just found the cookstove when her phone rang. The ring tone was 'Ride of the Valkyries.' She hadn't heard it for a while, but it sparked the same tightness in her chest as always, except worse, because her father wasn't supposed to have his phone. She picked up and said hello.

'My baby girl!' he said. Already, she could tell he was high. In the background, traffic hummed and honked.

'Where are you?' she said. 'Why aren't you in the centre?'

'I needed a break. I'm on vacation.'

'Where?' she repeated. He had to be somewhere in the city. He couldn't have been out very long or the centre would have phoned.

Her standard procedure when he called from random places was to start by pleading with him to come home, but that wasn't an option now. Even if she could somehow hide Ülle, Jari, and the baby, and even if she threw open all the doors and windows right away, the place wouldn't air out before he returned. Also, the dealer would notice. She needed to get him back to the centre.

'Dad, what are you doing?' she said. 'You've only got two more weeks of treatment.'

'I wanted to see my girl.'

That was bullshit. If he'd wanted to see her, he would have come home.

'Dad, you need to go back .'

'I can't,' he replied. 'I just broke out of the joint. Come meet me! We'll go for dinner.'

'I really, really need you back at the centre. Please? I'll never ask for anything again.'

'Good try,' he said. 'But I know what you're actually thinking.'

At these words, Regan froze. 'Dad, tell me that's just a figure of speech. Tell me you didn't – '

'Don't be ridiculous.'

He'd totally gone and done it.

'Dad, go back to the centre,' she said. 'If you're lost, I'll stay on the line and help you.'

'This conversation is boring,' he announced. 'I'm going to hang up.'

'Hold on,' she said. 'Just a second.'

She thought of sending Paul, but her father wouldn't stand for that. Then she thought of saying goodbye to him, loading the flatpacks in the car, and leaving him to fend for himself, sky-high in some sketchy part of town. The idea seemed so easy and elegant that she knew she'd never pull it off.

'Tell me where you are so I can get you,' she said.

'You'll stick me back in the centre.'

'Not if you don't want to be there,' she lied. 'We'll go for dinner, like you said.' There would be no dinner. 'You can come home after.' No way was he coming home.

She imagined the man in the van listening in on all of this. Well, if he was, he'd know that she had no choice but to go out.

'Where are you?' she tried again.

There was a pause. His phone grabbed the traffic sounds and amplified them.

'Near the lake,' he said. 'By that pool where we used to swim.'

'Sunnyside? Great. Go chill there until I get to you.'

'Okay.' As he spoke, she realized he was about to hang up.

'Wait, stay on – ' But she was too late.

She called him back. It went to voice mail. She texted him: '*Stay put. Call me.*' Then she turned to find Ülle standing there holding the baby.

'Van is gone,' Ülle said. 'It leaves two minutes ago.'

So maybe they weren't tapping her phone. If they were, why would they take off right then?

'I'm heading out by myself,' Regan said. 'My dad's in trouble. I have to get him to the place where he's been living. Then I'll come back and we'll leave, okay?'

Ülle looked unsure. 'What if man in mask returns?' she asked.

Regan thought for a second.

She went to the kitchen and eyed the knives. Too short; Ülle didn't have the reach. Regan descended to the recording studio and found her father's golf clubs. She selected the two with the biggest heads. They were left-handed, but she doubted it mattered.

'Here,' she said to Ülle in the living room, handing her one of the clubs and setting the other next to the door. 'Somebody comes in, you clobber them. While I'm gone, teach Jari how to swing it.'

When she went to grab the car keys from the candy bowl in the kitchen, a problem arose. The keys weren't there. She couldn't remember what she'd done with them. She checked her jacket. She checked her bedroom. She searched her jeans in the laundry hamper.

In the living room, she found Jari holding the baby and Ülle taking swings with the golf club, while a lamp lay broken on the floor.

'There is small accident,' said Ülle.

'Never mind,' said Regan. 'Have you seen my keys?' She went to Jari and patted down his pockets. He looked at her with a grin, as if it were a game. Then she checked the garage to see if she'd left them in the car.

That's when she discovered that the car had disappeared.

Everything else was in its place. Bikes, lawn mower, gardening tools. The garage door was closed. But where the Mustang had been parked was an empty space.

Had she left it outside? She returned to the living room and looked through the window. There was no car in sight.

Then she remembered the man in the mask. Maybe the noise that Paul had heard was the garage door opening or closing, her means of escape being driven away, the man ensuring that she stayed put and croaked as planned.

'Somebody stole the car,' she said to Ülle. 'That man who came in. Did you see him take the keys?'

Ülle shook her head, but it didn't matter. The car wasn't going to magically turn up again.

'We have to change the plan,' Regan said. She went to the window and saw that the van was still gone.

She could sneak out through the backyard, across the ravine. A couple of blocks away, there was a convenience store with a pay phone where she could call a cab.

'I'm still heading out,' she said. 'When I get back, we'll go to Lucinda's.' Lucinda had a car. Regan would convince her to lend it to her. Lucinda wasn't someone who'd call the cops when you told her it was a matter of life or death.

'Your ex?' said Ülle. 'How do we go to her?'

'Once it's dark, we'll walk. Her house is only a mile from here.'

'What if you do not come back today?' Ülle said.

'I'll come back.'

'What if they catch you?'

'Just stay put.' It wasn't the right answer, though. If they caught her, the dealer's goon might re-enter the house, and who knew what he'd do then.

She pulled out her phone to check the time.

'It's almost two,' she said. 'If I don't make it back by midnight, go to Lucinda's. I'll meet you there.'

'Not if they catch you,' Ülle said.

'They won't, all right?' The van could return at any minute. Regan needed to be gone. 'When you get there, hide in the garage. If it's locked, go to the back door and knock. Explain things to her. She'll help you. Just keep a few feet away, or you might freak her out.'

In fact, Regan had no clue how Lucinda would respond to the sight of flatpacks at her door, no matter how much distance they kept, but she didn't have any better ideas.

'Where is Lucinda's house?' asked Ülle.

Regan gave her the address, and Ülle looked like she was about to ask more questions. 'Google it,' Regan said, starting for the mudroom. 'I've got to go.'

She'd just laced her shoelaces when Ülle came up behind her.

'Promise again you will come back,' Ülle said. 'Promise you do not just leave us here.'

'I promise,' said Regan. 'I swear I won't.'

Ülle stepped in to hug her. Two hugs now. Maybe Regan should say something. She began to feel dizzy, and she wondered if the air in the house was finally taking effect. Or maybe she was just starting to pay for having consumed nothing that day but whisky, aspirin, and a spoonful of baby formula.

After Ülle released her, Regan murmured a goodbye. Then she went to the door and found Toodles there, wrapped in his bedsheet. Bending down, she moved him gently to the side before slipping out and sprinting across the yard. Her foot filled with pain, but she didn't stop.

Once she'd reached the trees, she turned to see what she'd left behind. The mudroom door was closed. Nobody in sight. The house looked peaceful, ordinary. For a second, the blinds on the mudroom window quivered, then went still.

If she'd waited a few more minutes, she would have heard Paul knock at the front door. She would have seen him circle the house, peering in the windows. She would have seen him try to call her and discover that his phone's battery had died. She would have seen his eyes glaze with fear as he spotted Ülle and Jari passing through the kitchen, Ülle holding the baby in her hands, looking for a place to hide.

Regan would have seen him arrive at the mudroom door and find it unlocked because she'd gone in haste. She would have been able to call out and let him know that she wasn't in the house. She could have stopped him from opening the door and gagging at the air inside. He wouldn't have taken off his T-shirt. He wouldn't have tied it around his mouth and gone in to save her.

As it was, she made her way down into the ravine and up the far slope, threading her way through patches of knotweed and purple briars with long thorns that drew her blood, as if to punish her for leaving, and when she turned again, the house was hidden from view.

FOUR

LETTER TO LITTLE ONE

Little one, let me tell you about Ülle and Jari in the Americas.

They fled their country with Mormor on the first day of November, carrying forged passports that identified them as citizens of another country, along with certificates declaring them worm-free. As far as Ülle knew, none of them had been tested. She feared how the border guards would receive such flim-flam documents, but Jari told her that everything had been arranged.

Early in the journey, crammed with Jari and Mormor into a compartment on a passenger train headed for the coast, Ülle learned that Mormor didn't like making small talk. She barely talked at all. Instead, her attention was given over to knitting a blue-and-purple scarf. In her youth, she'd been a national champion in the shot put, and, as Jari explained to Ülle, she'd taken up knitting during competitions as a way to stay occupied between throws. Since becoming the head of her family, Mormor had made each of its members a scarf or cap in the clan colours. If you wore one, it stopped hoodlums and police officers from accosting you, because they knew you were under Mormor's wing. Ülle wondered whether the scarf Mormor knitted now was meant for her. She wondered if it would have any power in the Americas.

Once they reached the coast, there was a voyage by ocean liner across the North Atlantic, wracked by storms. Ülle took to her bed with fever, and Jari said that perhaps her sickness was for the best, because Mormor had banned them from speaking with people, not wanting their accents to raise suspicions. He stayed by Ülle's side, mopping her brow, offering her sips of water, and sharing nuggets of information from his reading about the Americas. He also told her that he'd taken over the responsibility of testing Mormor's acid levels and administering her shots.

Like Snaut used to do, said Ülle, and Jari voiced his surprise. He hadn't thought that Mormor would tell Ülle about Snaut.

After ten vomitous days, they reached the Americas, disembarking at Oyster Island. Just before the inspection booths, a pair of men in ill-fitting uniforms led them away from the other passengers. Ülle, still woozy with sickness, was terrified, but Jari and Mormor seemed at ease as the men guided them to a skiff and ferried them to the mainland. Once there, the men departed, and the three of them took a taxi to the station, where they boarded a train heading north to the city of Tkaronto.

At their destination, a balding man with the crepe-paper skin of a lifelong smoker ushered them into a limousine. Jari explained that the man had worked for their family in the old country before emigrating years ago. Now he was to serve as Mormor's aide, living in the basement apartment of the house that had been acquired for them. Ülle stared at the back of the man's head, with its patch of thinning hair too black to be real, and wondered about the life he'd been living, that he could so readily abandon it to serve Mormor. In the weeks ahead, Jari and Mormor would refer to him only as Driver.

As they crossed the city, Ülle marvelled at the crowds of people on the sidewalks, all going about placidly in a land without the worm. They carried plump shopping bags and wore clothes that looked brand-new. A city of plenty. Upon reaching the house, Ülle marvelled once more. It was half the size of Mormor's old place but still enormous, and it sat in a neighbourhood called Rosedale, an enclave of mansions set off from the rest of the city by deep ravines, as if nature had conspired with the residents to keep out those who couldn't afford to belong. In the late-autumn breeze, the few remaining leaves on the oaks lining the boulevards seemed to rustle in a genteel, orderly way, like money being counted. Driver told them that, a few years earlier, Rosedale had been the only neighbourhood in Tkaronto not to change its name to one from before the arrival of Columbus.

He gave them a perfunctory tour of the house, and then Mormor, after claiming a room on the second floor as her office, disappeared into it, while Jari went with Driver to inspect what Driver called the perimeter. Ülle was left to unpack her belongings in her and Jari's bedroom, which was sparsely furnished and undecorated. She didn't have much to add: a change of clothes, a few toiletries, and a pair of fleecy slippers that had once been her brother's. She kept her secret pills hidden in the pocket of her winter coat.

Once she had put away her things, she realized that she didn't know what came next. In the old country, she and Jari had decided that she would study bookkeeping. She liked numbers, took pleasure in the neatness of things adding up, and Mormor had approved of the plan after Jari suggested to her that Ülle could help with the family's accounts. Also, the courses were online, so Ülle wouldn't have to speak English out in the world and risk being exposed. Jari had given her a laptop; she could, she supposed, get started right away. But she was underslept and still coughing out the last of her sickness, so she crawled into bed and fell asleep.

When she awoke, the house lay silent. Down the hall, Mormor's office door was closed. Ülle wandered the building, half in search of Jari, half taking in the house. She examined the bookless library, the kitchen with its pots and pans still wrapped in plastic on the countertops. When she looked out the parlour window, she saw Driver smoking in the garage's open doorway. She went out to ask him about Jari and was told he'd gone downtown on business. Then, in an offhand manner, Driver added that Mormor expected dinner at six o'clock. He said that she'd given instructions for Ülle not to leave the property by herself, so he would take her wherever she needed to go for supplies.

Seeing her look of consternation, he added that it was Mormor's habit to be careful in all things.

Ülle nodded, trying to mask her anger. She understood how this family worked, how Mormor's decisions weren't to be questioned, but Ülle hadn't received the slightest warning, neither from Mormor nor from Jari, that she was being returned to domestic service.

In the kitchen, the cupboards were bare. She made a list of things to buy, then spent an hour searching online for stores that sold them, before asking Driver to take her there. On the way, he hummed along with the music from a portable radio in his lap, which was tuned to the only station still broadcasting from the old country. It played folk songs that Ülle had never heard in her girlhood but that had regained popularity in the time of the worm, when people were grateful for reminders of the past.

Their first stop was in Oronhyatekha, a neighbourhood south of Rosedale filled with dispensaries, hock shops, and takeout restaurants. A deli there promised on its website that it sold pork pâté. As Ülle entered, a bell above the door tinkled, and she felt the eyes of the woman behind the counter fix on her. Ülle hurried to the refrigerator aisle, eager to escape the woman's gaze.

Having no luck finding the pâté, she noticed someone restocking a shelf of canned foods at the back of the store: a tall, gaunt man with bushy red eyebrows and a pointed chin, dressed in clothes resembling pyjamas. His hands and face shone silver, and from the side of his neck, just below the hairline, protruded a little black nozzle.

Ülle had seen videos of flatpacked people. She'd watched them being cared for by American families, cavorting with dogs and children, strolling beaches and forest paths, wearing smiles that unsettled her because they looked so much more uncomplicated than smiles had any right to be. This man in the store was the first flatpacked person she'd encountered in the flesh, and as he went about his work, studying each can that he set on the shelf as if to confirm that it was identical to its companions, he smiled in the same unsettling way. Eventually, he turned to face her, and his smile grew.

Good afternoon, he said. How are you, my countrywoman?

Ülle froze. Was there something in her face, her cheekbones, that gave her away? Perhaps 'my countrywoman' was simply a term of greeting here.

He started in her direction, spreading his arms as if to embrace her. She took a step back, wanting to flee but worried about the attention it would bring.

Then another voice came from behind her.

Is he bothering you?

It was the woman from the counter, holding a broom.

I told you, no talking to customers, the woman said to the man. She strode past Ülle and swung the broom at him, catching him on the thigh and eliciting a yip of pain.

You have to be firm with them, the woman told Ülle. Then, to the man she said, Come on, back to work! She hit him again, higher this time.

Ülle hurried back up the aisle.

Wait, the woman called after her. Don't go acting all offended.

Ülle didn't stop.

In the limousine, Ülle couldn't control her breathing. Driver wanted to know what was wrong.

The flatpacked people, she said. Are they everywhere?

He nodded.

Do you not – she began, then wondered if her words would be reported to Mormor. Do you not find yourself wanting to help them? she asked.

Help them? Driver said, sounding suspicious. What's to be done?

Before she could answer, he started the car and took them back into traffic.

Ülle had been ambitious in her dinner plans, setting out to make stuffed eggs and paprika chicken with polenta, dishes that her mother had served guests she wanted to impress, but by the time they returned to the house, there was hardly time to prepare the meal. As she went about her work, she listened to Mormor pace the office overhead, making the floorboards groan as the ocean liner had in storms.

At five to six, with the chicken still in the oven, Jari entered the kitchen, kissed her on the cheek, and asked how the food was coming. His voice had a strained jollity, a hint of guilt, as if he'd known that this was how she would spend her day. A few minutes later, Mormor descended and sat at the table expectantly, ignoring the fact that Ülle had set places in the dining room. In the end, the eggs were hard, the polenta lumpy, the chicken tough as leather, and when Jari offered his compliments, Ülle assumed he was being sarcastic. Mormor didn't say a word.

It seemed like a disaster but turned out to be life, because whatever Mormor thought of the dinner, she expected more like it in the days that followed. There was no help from Jari; each morning, he left on unnamed business, not returning until dinner. Soon it became clear that Mormor expected Ülle to clean the house as well. Mormor could surely afford to hire someone, but Ülle understood, without it being said aloud, that until she added to the family, she would have to earn her keep in other ways.

She still took her secret pills. Before leaving the old country, she had acquired enough of them to last six months. Whenever she considered abandoning them, she pictured a frog-sized Mormor inside her, all blue veins and fetal muscle, and a rage boiled up at Mormor and at Jari, too, at the thought that what they wanted was a breeding mare.

If you find Ülle's wilfulness in this matter perverse, little one, then what will you think when I tell you that her treason wasn't even necessary, because since leaving their country, she and Jari hadn't once made love? At night in bed, he pleaded exhaustion or headaches, or he said that Tkaronto's damp cold made his guts seize. He complained about the girth of the city's toilet seats, claiming that they were sized for people with American asses, and that the thought of falling into the bowl made him nervous, so that since they'd immigrated, he hadn't once, as his uncle Gunnar used to put it, sent a timber down the flume.

Given the state of Jari's intestines, it was hard to imagine him wanting to consume anything, but each day Ülle awoke to find the leftovers from the previous night's dinner vanished from the fridge. He always denied eating them, saying it must have been Mormor or Driver. The lie was so bald-faced that Ülle almost laughed each time he repeated it, but he never cracked a smile. Never once did he acknowledge what both of them were surely thinking: that constipation and surges in appetite were symptoms of the worm.

Little one, if you thought that your lover might be dying, and if he seemed unwilling to discuss it, what would you do? Some people would say that Ülle was wrong not to insist on a conversation. But not speaking had always been her and Jari's way. With looks and caresses, they communicated most of what was necessary. For the rest, they counted on the fact that they had both known the same losses, heartaches, fears. Talk of these things, Ülle felt certain, would only cause more pain. The same was true of the worm. If it was in him, nothing could be done – nothing except flatpacking, and he'd already told her what he thought about that. More talk would be useless. You couldn't talk the worm out of somebody. You couldn't speak people back to life.

So she kept to cooking and cleaning, and although it might seem that these things would be easy enough with only three people to care for, there was always more to do. Most days, her busyness kept her from dwelling on Jari and the worm, but during errands with Driver, she couldn't avoid reminders, because even though she never returned to the deli in Oronhyatekha, there were flatpacked people working in many stores, and she saw others on the streets, often toting things for their companions, sometimes out ahead of them on leashes. In Rosedale, she saw flatpacked people playing with toddlers in the park, blithely tolerating the children's happy screams, while nearby nannies checked their phones. Sometimes Ülle liked to imagine that once she and Jari had gained legal standing in the country and were living under their own roof, they would adopt a flatpacked person. They would adopt more than one, if possible, and give them the best lives they could have.

Those were Ülle's first two weeks in Tkaronto. Then, one afternoon, Driver appeared in the kitchen with a summons from Mormor. Jari hadn't yet returned home that day, so there was no chance to ask him what his grandmother wanted or to strategize about how to act. Ülle simply went to Mormor's office door and knocked, and Mormor's voice told her to enter.

Inside, the overhead light was off and the windows were cloaked by heavy curtains. The only source of illumination was a banker's lamp on the desk where Mormor sat knitting. Her frizz of white hair had been battened down by a few pins. She never bothered with makeup or jewellery, and she was wearing what Ülle now knew to be one of the few drab dresses constituting her wardrobe. Each was as shapeless as the last, but beneath their fabric, her muscles bulged and rolled.

Come here, Mormor said, and Ülle approached the desk. There was no chair for her.

Tell me what you think I'm knitting, Mormor said.

Ülle leaned forward, hoping that it was a scarf and that this was the moment in which Mormor would welcome her into the family. All she saw was a patch of stitches tethered to a ball of purple yarn.

I don't know, she said.

It's for a baby, said Mormor.

Ülle straightened. If some other old woman had been sitting across the desk, Ülle would have made a joke about the woman being too old for a bun in the oven. Now, she didn't speak.

So you see, said Mormor, I'm doing my part for the family. It's time that you did yours.

I've been trying, said Ülle. I mean, Jari and I have been trying together.

So why have you failed? said Mormor.

Ülle thought of explaining about Jari's difficulties. She told herself that she'd be doing it not to avoid blame but to help him; that Mormor might coax him into discussing the worm. But if she told Mormor, he would feel betrayed.

I don't know, was all she said.

Well, we know you can have a child, said Mormor. But don't you think it would be best to see if your parts are still working?

Ülle felt her cheeks flare. Mormor returned her gaze to the knitting.

I'm sending you to a doctor, she said. Driver will take you tomorrow morning.

Ülle opened her mouth to object. As she did so, though, she discovered that she had no real argument to make in protest, so she didn't speak. A moment later, the resumption of the needles' clicking told her that she'd been dismissed.

Only after leaving the room did she realize that Mormor needn't have informed her of the appointment personally. She could have had Driver or Jari deliver the news. Perhaps she'd shared it herself so that Ülle might confide her hopes and frustrations with respect to conceiving. Or perhaps she'd wanted to see if she could detect a resistance in Ülle to the mission of family increase.

A visit to the doctor would almost certainly bring a blood test, and the prospect threw Ülle into a state of dread. If she had the worm, the test would reveal it, which was frightening enough. What she didn't know was whether such a test would reveal the traces of her secret pills. She wanted to see online whether her fears were justified, but ever since moving to the Americas, she had worried that Mormor was monitoring her computer use. Hadn't Driver said it was Mormor's habit to be careful?

That evening, when Jari returned, Ülle told him of her imminent appointment. He seemed unsurprised, and she realized with bitterness that Mormor must have already informed him.

You needn't worry, he said. You're healthy as a horse.

What if the doctor asks about us? she said. About our relations?

Just tell the truth, he replied. I'll look after things with Mormor.

That night, he fell asleep in seconds while Ülle tossed and turned. She imagined begging the doctor not to tell Mormor about the pills. She imagined running away.

It seemed that she had only just reached unconsciousness when she awoke in the darkness to find Jari gone. After a few minutes passed without him returning, she went downstairs. He stood hunched over the kitchen table, the roast beef from dinner unwrapped before him, wolfing down strips of meat so jagged that it seemed he had torn them off with his fingers. His eyes were bloodshot, his skin pallid, and gravy darkened the corners of his lips.

I'm famished, he said. I can't stop eating. It has to be the worm.

Have you felt other symptoms? she asked, trying not to show her panic.

The constipation, he replied.

Nothing else? she said.

He stuck another strip of beef in his mouth and fell silent. She knew he must be thinking, as she was, of their failure to conceive.

Perhaps you should be tested, she said.

What difference would it make? he muttered.

The result could be negative, she said.

And if it's positive? he asked.

She took a deep breath, knowing she was on the brink of forbidden territory.

Then you could consider being flatpacked, she said.

He gave her a long stare.

Testing is dangerous, he said. If the government found out I had the worm, I'd be deported.

There must be ways to be tested safely, she said.

It doesn't matter anyhow, he said. You know what Mormor thinks of flatpacking. What I think, too.

She felt her desperation growing.

You told me you didn't like the idea of flatpacks being sent to the Americas, she said. But we're here now. You wouldn't have to live with strangers. I'd take care of you. One day, when they find a cure for the worm –

Stop it, he said.

They'll find a way to reverse the flatpacking, too, she said. And then –

I said stop it, he said, so loudly that they both froze, listening for the sounds of Mormor stirring above them.

I don't understand, Ülle whispered. Why can't you allow yourself to hope?

He slumped forward, his face falling into shadow.

I hoped for my parents and friends, he said. For my aunts and uncles. My cousins. My wife and daughter.

You don't have the worm, she insisted. You eat like this because you feel guilty that you're still alive.

A great tiredness came over her.

Come to bed, she said, reaching out her hand.

Not yet, he said, pointing at the roast beef. I have to finish this.

He was still down there when she fell asleep, and when she woke up, he had already gone for the day.

Even before Driver appeared at breakfast to tell her that they needed to leave for her appointment, she was too nervous to eat. She went with him like a prisoner condemned, sitting in the back of the limousine as he drove her to a strip mall on the city's west side. In the parking lot, he gestured toward a grubby storefront with its windows boarded up. It felt like a trap, like Mormor had decided there was no room in the family for a barren ex-governess, but Ülle could see no option other than to go where Driver pointed.

The store, when she reached it, was locked tight. She pressed a buzzer by the door. Footsteps approached from within, the door swung open, and a short, dark-haired woman not much older than herself, wearing street clothes and a stethoscope around her neck, ushered her inside.

The space was narrow and nearly empty. Drop cloths and paint buckets littered the floor, while long fluorescent tubes buzzed overhead. The woman introduced herself as Dr. Rama-chandran and led Ülle to the back, where an examining table stood behind a padded office divider. The doctor asked Ülle to sit on the table. Then she asked her questions about her family's medical conditions, her cycle, her sexual history. Ülle assumed that her answers would be reported to Mormor, so she told the truth about everything – everything except the pills, and how often she and Jari made love.

The doctor asked her to undress and lie on the table. It juddered beneath her weight, and the metal top pressed coldly against her back. The doctor checked every part of her, handling her flesh with latex gloves and a wordless efficiency.

Nothing unusual, she said at the end. Then she announced her intention to draw blood.

While the doctor tied a rubber tube around Ülle's arm, she thought of confessing, pleading with the woman not to betray her. Before she could bring herself to speak, a needle found her vein, and the first vial filled with blood.

Are you testing for the worm? she asked.

I can't discuss it, the doctor said.

How long until the results? Ülle asked.

A few days, said the doctor, and Ülle realized that there was still time to run away.

Once she had her clothes back on, the doctor showed her to the door. Just as Ülle was about to step outside, the doctor spoke.

Are they taking good care of you? she asked.

What do you mean? said Ülle, on her guard.

I mean, are they looking after you? said the doctor. Are you happy?

Ülle frowned.

Of course, she replied. I'm very fortunate.

The doctor murmured her assent to this idea. Then she opened the door for her. Ülle walked out and discovered that while she had been inside, it had begun to snow. Fat grey flakes wheeled through the air and melted on the parking-lot asphalt before they'd even had the chance to settle.

On the drive home, it occurred to her that if the doctor cared so much as to ask how she was being treated, she might have also agreed to keep Ülle's secret. It was too late, though. Ülle wished that she knew whether the test would detect the pills. She decided that when she was out with Driver the next day, she'd find an excuse to go into a drugstore and ask a pharmacist.

She didn't get the chance. First thing the next morning, Mormor summoned her to her office again. Without bothering to greet her, she asked what had happened at the doctor's.

What do you mean? said Ülle in alarm.

Mormor slammed down her knitting. The force of her fists on the desk travelled to the floor and up through Ülle's legs.

What did the doctor say to you? Mormor demanded.

She asked about my health, said Ülle.

Did she mention Jari? said Mormor.

Not once, said Ülle. Did she see him, too?

Mormor ignored the question.

Think back, she said. Tell me every detail.

Ülle did her best to recount the appointment, repeating all the doctor's questions but the last ones at the door.

That's everything? Mormor said once she'd finished.

Yes, she said, feeling Mormor's eyes bore into her.

Go then, said Mormor. When you see Jari, tell him I want to talk.

In the hour that followed, Ülle went about the house cleaning and tidying mindlessly, alive to every creak from Mormor's office. She had no way to contact Jari. For all she knew, her fate had been decided. She considered making her way downtown and stealing aboard a train, starting with nothing in some other city, trying to speak without an accent.

Just before lunchtime, Jari returned. He never came home so early. When she greeted him, he barely acknowledged her.

I must talk with Mormor, he said, heading for the stairs.

This morning she called me into her office, Ülle said.

I know, he replied. We'll talk later. I can't keep her waiting.

Ülle watched from the landing as he stepped into Mormor's office. For twenty minutes, she tried to keep herself busy. When he re-emerged, he led her to their bedroom and closed the door behind them.

The doctor has disappeared, he said in a low voice. Run off.

Why would she do that? Ülle whispered.

Mormor thinks I told her to vanish at my appointment, he said.

You saw her? Ülle said. Why would you tell her to run off?

Because she wasn't safe, he said.

Why not? Ülle asked, and he didn't respond.

Ülle's first thought was her blood test. The doctor wanted to protect her by guarding the result. But running off was too extreme. And why would Ülle's test result make the doctor unsafe? There must be another explanation.

Then Ülle realized what it was. In the same moment, Jari gathered her into his arms, holding her so tightly that the breath went from her.

You'll always be here for me, no matter what? he said.

She was right then. He'd been tested. It was his result that had caused the trouble. The doctor's knowledge of it would make her a liability in Mormor's eyes.

You warned the doctor that she was in danger? Ülle said.

He squeezed her a little harder.

Once he'd left the room, she fetched her pills, took them to the bathroom, and flushed them down the toilet, vowing to stick things out with him, even on the final day when the worm made its debut.

A week passed. Mormor didn't summon Ülle again, and no one spoke further of test results or medical appointments. Nobody mentioned the doctor. Jari didn't discuss his health either, but he kept vanishing from bed at night, leaving Ülle to discover the empty fridge each morning, and at every meal he helped himself to seconds and thirds, though anyone could see he was growing thin. She knew that he would take it as treachery if she so much as made a comment.

The long hours indoors became unbearable. As they reached December, the sunlight drained bit by bit from either end of the day. It was dark when Jari left in the morning and dark when he returned for dinner. The house was cold and drafty. The rooms echoed with Mormor's pacing and the clang of the basement furnace. When Ülle told Jari that she needed to start taking walks in the neighbourhood alone sometimes, she expected to be rebuked, but he only shrugged and said, Go then, you aren't a hostage.

The next afternoon, she went out and discovered that a cold snap had left sheets of dark ice on the ground. As she walked with her hands stuffed in her pockets, she had to keep her eyes on her footing, but she glanced up every so often, somehow imagining that she might spot the doctor seeking her out, wanting to offer help. Ülle entertained a fantasy of running away with her and Jari. The worm was unpredictable; Jari might have months, even years. Maybe in time, untethered from Mormor, he would come around to flatpacking.

She was passing by the playground in a deserted park when she looked up and saw the last person she would have expected in that place. It was an old man from her village. Cata, the professor. He stood at the bottom of the slide as if having just descended it. He had seen her, too, and he started walking in her direction.

In her village, Cata was famous. He'd grown up quiet and friendless, reading all the books in the public library, winning every prize at school. In time, he'd left and become a chemistry professor, inventing a growth hormone that made him very rich. It was said that he owned property in half a dozen countries, yet upon his retirement, he moved back to the village, demolishing his parents' ramshackle cottage to build his own house of steel and glass. She'd seen him in the stores, speaking to the shop-keepers with a stilted affability, as if straining to fit in. He was a lifelong bachelor. Even before the plague, people gossiped about where his money would go. When the worm overran the village, he disappeared.

Now here he was, his beard gone and silver jowls exposed. The flatpacking had removed his face's finer wrinkles. She recognized him only by his owlish eyes and the exuberance with which he smiled at her.

Hello! he said. A beautiful day, yes?

She couldn't tell whether he remembered her or was only being friendly. There seemed to be no one else around. Then a voice hissed at her from behind.

Come away from him, it said. Come over here!

She turned to see another old man sitting on a bench, clutching a bamboo cane. Grey hair grazed his shoulders, and he wore eyeglasses with thick purple frames. As she approached, he shouted at Cata to stay in the playground.

You shouldn't stand near him, the man whispered. Haven't you heard the news?

Ülle shook her head, wary of speaking.

They're dangerous, the man said. Some vapour from them has been killing people.

He sounded quite distraught. In the playground, Cata returned to the slide and climbed its ladder.

They're being rounded up, the man said. You're supposed to call the police department and keep them outside until help arrives.

His throat seemed to close around the words. The mention of the police made Ülle anxious, but she felt it would be wrong just to leave the man, so she sat down beside him, telling herself she'd stay only a minute.

I haven't smelled anything, he said. I feel fine. But the neighbour came to check on me today and said she'd made the call. I don't blame her, she has small children. She told me to take him to the park, so here we are.

His eyes grew watery. The two of them watched Cata go down the slide a few times, laughing as he went. Ülle thought of telling the man that this was Cata the professor, the most famous person from her village.

She didn't need to call the police, the man said dolefully. I live alone with him. Nobody would miss me. And he's sweet as can be, never causes trouble.

The man burst into tears.

What am I going to do? he whispered.

In the distance, sirens began to wail. Ülle hurried to her feet. The man was crying loudly enough for Cata to rush over. Taking Ülle's place on the bench, he threw his arms around him.

Don't cry, Cata said, stroking the man's face. What's wrong? Don't cry. It's all right. Don't cry.

She was almost out of the park when the police van jumped the curb and churned past her across the grass. It stopped beside the playground, and the back doors burst open, disgorging half a dozen figures encased head to toe in yellow suits.

The man with the cane started their way. One of them broke off from the others to confront him. The rest advanced toward Cata. She could make out his smile as he stood and waved at them. Then they halted, all but one, who continued on toward him, arm extended. Ülle couldn't tell if the figure held a weapon. She waited for a gunshot that didn't come. Instead, Cata stretched out his arm in turn, and he and the figure walked back to the van together, hand in hand, Cata still smiling, his new friend helping him into the vehicle.

These proceedings were watched by the man with the cane as though he were frozen in place. Perhaps the person in the suit beside him had said that things would go more easily if he didn't make a fuss. But as the van doors closed with Cata and the rest of them inside, the old man began to shout and hobble toward the vehicle, the person beside him keeping pace. Once they reached the van, the old man banged his cane desperately against the side, while the person in the suit climbed into the vehicle. The van shifted into gear and drove away.

That night, as she told Jari what had happened, he listened with seeming disinterest, like a store manager receiving a complaint from a customer known to be quarrelsome. When she finished, he said that they'd been dealing with this issue for some time, but it had become public knowledge only in the past few days. The problem wasn't with every flatpack, just the newest ones. They suspected a flaw in the manufacturing process, one that triggered off-gassing once the flatpacks were inflated. There had been some bad situations. The adoption program had been cancelled, and now the government was rounding up all the flatpacks, old and new alike.

What will they do with them? Ülle asked.

Jari said that he didn't know, but that the factory in the old country had been shut down, at least officially. Unofficially, there was still money to be made. People of means who learned that they had the worm were, by and large, willing to gamble on a solution to the off-gassing eventually being found. In the meantime, they didn't care if they weren't adopted by Americans. They just wanted to be spared from the worm. His last surviving cousin, who remained in the old country overseeing the factory, had told him that every day new flatpacks were being stacked in the warehouse like kindling.

FIVE

HENCHMAN

In the back seat of the cab, Regan kept turning to see if they were being tailed. Halfway through the ride to the waterfront, she spotted a beige van approaching. The vehicle passed by them and sped off. A second later, her phone rang. It was the supervisor at the treatment centre, wanting to let Regan know that her father had left without telling anybody. The woman said she was concerned, when all she probably cared about was not getting sued. Regan said not to worry, he'd been in touch, and she'd have him back there right away. As she hung up, she hoped she hadn't sounded as awful as she felt. The whisky in her stomach sloshed with every bump in the road.

Two years had passed since she'd last rescued him. Back then, he still talked of making music, but all he really did was play covers one Monday a month at a gimcrack Irish pub owned by an old beer buddy whom he claimed to be doing a favour. The night the guy called Regan, though, asking if she could pick her father up, the disdain in his voice suggested that the favour ran in the other direction. Once she got there, her father's jumpiness made it clear that he hadn't just been drinking.

At the parking lot for the pool, there was no sign of him. When she asked the driver to wait while she had a look around, he sucked his teeth and asked to be paid for the ride so far.

'My philosophy,' he said, although she hadn't asked to hear it, 'is that you aren't just hiring my car, you're hiring my life. So when you make me wait, you put a whole life on hold.'

She didn't think it sounded like a great philosophy for a cab driver.

A cool wind blew off the lake, slinging waves over the break-wall that ran parallel to the shoreline park. A row of willows stood heavy with yellow catkins. From behind her came the thrum of traffic on Lake Shore Boulevard. It was mid-afternoon, with a month to go before the end of the school year, and the paved fitness trail was nearly deserted. A shirtless man with cartoonish muscles wobbled along on rollerblades, while a black poodle lacking a visible companion sniffed its way down the thin gravel beach.

The pool was closed. A sign blamed renovations. Next door was a playground with a jungle gym, a swing set, and someone in a baggy green sweatshirt sitting on the end of a teeter-totter, legs splayed. Only when he waved to her did she know for sure it was her dad.

'My knight in shining armour,' he exclaimed.

'Come on, I've got a cab waiting,' she shouted as she approached him. 'I ordered it just for you. I said to myself, no stanky old Uber for a father of mine.'

It was amazing how quickly, in his presence, this version of her sprang into action. Dealing with his freak-outs, she seemed to muster a self-possession that she could never manage on her own.

His brow furrowed. 'Where's the Mustang?' he said. 'I'm not getting in a cab. I want my car.'

He dismounted the teeter-totter, and she saw that his pupils had swallowed his irises.

'The car's in the shop,' she said. 'What's the difference to you anyhow? You weren't going to be driving it.' Losing his licence was one of the reasons he'd ended up at the centre.

'I don't trust that guy,' he said.

'The cabbie? You haven't even met him.'

'He's a cheat. He plans to charge you double. I mean, his father beat him, and he's got five kids, but – '

She couldn't believe it. He wasn't on just any old kind of high.

'You got horseshoed, didn't you?' she cried.

'Come on, you know me better than that,' he replied, averting his eyes.

How had he managed it? At the centre, he wasn't supposed to have money. Maybe he'd come here because one of his turdpipe musician friends lived nearby.

'If you didn't get horseshoed, let's see your back,' she said.

When she reached to yank at his sweatshirt, he jerked away.

'I know you're angry – ' he began.

'Dad, that shit doesn't actually let you read minds. We go through this every time.' While he was on the stuff, though, it wouldn't matter what she said. 'Let's just get you to the centre. You can snoop into everybody's thoughts there.'

He shook his head. 'I'm not going back.'

'Why not?'

'I don't want to talk about it.'

She puffed out her cheeks. 'Dad, you only have two weeks left.' Except now that he'd got horseshoed, they'd probably make him start over.

'I never wanted to go there,' he said. 'You're the one who wanted it.'

Her face filled with blood. 'We all agreed. You and me and Mom.'

It wasn't the whole truth. Her mother had agreed only after he raided Regan's college fund. Even then, Mom hadn't come home. She'd said it was up to Regan to make the arrangements.

'You were depressed,' Regan reminded him. 'You couldn't sleep, you were hallucinating.' You were always coked up, too, she almost added, but the centre had said not to dwell on past behaviours.

He looked toward the horizon, where the lake topped out in a jittery line. Then he glanced at the parking lot again. She followed his gaze and saw that the cab was gone.

'I want to go home,' he said.

She'd figured he might say that.

'You can't,' she replied. 'The house is being fumigated.' Seeing the look on his face, she added, 'It's just bedbugs. Like, a couple of them. But we can't go in for a few days.'

'Where are you staying?' he asked. When she started to say something, he stopped her. 'Don't tell me. Lucinda's, right?'

She rolled her eyes, then decided to go with it. 'How did you know? For somebody who isn't on horseshoe, you're quite a mind reader.'

He beamed with satisfaction before his expression turned quizzical. 'I thought she broke up with you,' he said.

Regan glared at him, and he shrugged.

'Fine, so I'll get a hotel room,' he said. 'Did you bring my wallet?'

She told him that she hadn't. He grimaced and reached to scratch at his back.

'What's the matter?' she said. 'Is it the horseshoe? Let me see. It could be infected.'

'I don't know – '

'I promise not to get all preachy. If you can read my mind, you know I'm telling the truth, right?'

He stared at her, right between the eyes, and her brain started to itch, like he was actually in there, rooting around. Then he rucked up his sweatshirt for her.

Even before she saw the tattoos, she noticed the flab. For years, he'd been skinny from all the drugs. Not anymore. The centre had promised that he'd eat well and exercise every day, but it looked like he'd done only the first of those.

The horseshoes were up near his shoulders. There were almost a dozen, each the size and colour of a plum, some sideways, some upside down, like stamps in a passport. At least he always got them where nobody would see them. If he didn't watch it, though, he was going to turn into one of those horseshoe addicts who ended up in jail for stalking strangers, trying to eavesdrop on their thoughts, hoping to pirate their banking passwords. Or he'd gamble away the rest of her college fund playing poker, always baffled when the other guys turned out not to have the cards he thought they did. Men on horseshoe propositioned women without taking no for an answer, convinced that the women were secretly falling for their charms. And then there were the ones who believed they could overhear everybody thinking horrible things about them. Some of those folks didn't handle it so well.

Regan had no trouble finding the latest horseshoe. The skin on which it had been branded was still raised and bloody.

'How does it look?' he said.

'Fugly,' she replied.

She didn't like tattoos. You started out in life with your body this flawless, fragile thing, and you had a duty to keep that thing as perfect as you could. It wasn't easy. Stress fractures, mono, low iron, amenorrhea, flu, fungal infections, UTIs, HPV, plantar fasciitis. She was always fucking herself up by accident. Why would she fuck herself up on purpose, too?

Her father reached over his shoulder to trace the newest horseshoe with an index finger, following it from one branch to the other.

'You know the shape's symbolic, right?' he said. 'To show how we're all connected.'

'Who said that? The asshat who put it on you?'

'Seriously, how does it look?'

'Bleeding a little.'

'That's okay. It always does that.'

Then he tensed up.

'What is it?' she demanded.

'I was just thinking,' he replied. 'About how other people can get some of the effect from touching it.'

'Yeah, you told me before.' She drew away a bit.

'Why don't you do it?' he said.

'Dad, we've been through this.' Whenever he was strung out, he turned evangelical for the stuff.

'You could read my thoughts,' he said. 'It might be good for you to see what's going on in your old dad's brain.'

The idea made her skin crawl.

'I mean, it's all nice stuff,' he said. 'The stuff about you anyway.'

'If there's something you want to tell me, just say it.'

He opened his mouth to speak but stopped himself. 'Some things are hard to put into words.'

'Is this about your reason for leaving the centre?'

He let his sweatshirt fall down over his back. 'That's not a secret,' he said. 'I was, I don't know – '

'You were what?'

'I was lonely.'

'Oh.' She'd been hoping for complaints about the food or the orderlies, something she could have argued about, promised to fix.

'Sorry,' he said. 'It's stupid, I shouldn't have told you – '

'It isn't stupid.' There wasn't time for a heart-to-heart, though. 'I'll visit you more often, okay?'

'It's not about visits. If you could see what's going on with me – '

'I'm not getting anywhere near your horseshoe.' The last thing she needed was to be stoned and thinking she could read people's minds.

'The hit would only last a few seconds.'

'Dad, why are you always trying to talk your child into taking drugs?'

He gave a chuckle, like what she'd said wasn't an exact description of reality. In a second, she'd be yelling at him, and what had yelling ever accomplished? It wouldn't help her get home any faster. In these situations, she knew what worked. She needed to give in, humour him, then use her surrender as leverage.

'Okay, you win,' she said. 'I'll touch the horseshoe.'

He broke into a smile, looking so happy that it pained her.

'But only if you make a promise,' she added. 'After, you'll go back to the centre.'

His expression soured.

'Do we have a deal?' she said.

He gave his head a shake, like he was clearing an Etch A Sketch, then turned upbeat again. 'Sure, deal.'

He'd agreed way too easily, but what could she do?

'Come here then,' she said.

Once more, he hiked up his sweatshirt. The new horseshoe looked spongy with blood. She thought of dirty needles, hepatitis. She pictured making a fool of herself with the first stranger who came along, telling them she could see their pedo fantasies. Maybe the horseshoe wouldn't have an effect, though. If the off-gassing didn't, why would a tattoo?

'I just put my hand on it?' she said, and he nodded.

'Five seconds should do the trick.'

Regan placed her fingers on the horseshoe and felt the wetness of his blood. Then she whipped her hand away and wiped it on the grass.

She was waiting to see if there'd be a drib of good feeling when she felt the kick. It struck her in the back of the neck and fireworked through her: a charge of elation, a hot fizz. She scrunched her eyes to take it in. When she opened them, she was flat on her back, staring at clouds.

'You're okay,' said her father. 'Take deep breaths. Go with it.'

The fizz had started to crest when she went rushing into him. Though she still lay on the ground, she had the sensation of their bodies smashing together, like the circles from two spotlights blending on a wall. The next thing she knew, she was looking out from his eyes, down at herself. She saw other faces overlaying hers: her mother's, her grandparents', younger than she'd ever known them. She heard an old-timey tune she didn't recognize, but played in his style, all capoed cross-picking, hitting the strings hard. Then the music slid beneath his cramp of worry. Words that weren't words arrived in swirls of mood and memory. *What happened to my little girl? No more races, hardly any muscle. Used to be so fast. How many times did I tell her, calories in have to equal calories burned? Didn't I say listen to your body? Doesn't care what I tell her. Always goes it alone, and she doesn't even know how to look after herself.*

From somewhere outside his head came his other voice.

'It's working, isn't it? You can see my thoughts?'

'It's too much,' she whispered.

'Hang on. It won't last.'

His brain kept up its tumble. *Throat's sore. Need a drink. People are always leaving. Bet her mother's not even worried. Sickness and health until death do you part – or a highfalutin posting. Doesn't matter to her what happens to us.*

Regan needed it to stop.

A rill of static trickled down the middle of his thoughts. Slowly, their lodgement in her loosened, and then all at once he was sluiced away, dragged out until he was so far gone that he became a separate person standing over her.

She propped herself up on her elbows and listened to the screech of gulls, a bike bell ringing on the fitness trail, waves exploding against the breakwall. Each thing sounded discrete and of itself. Her father asked her if she was okay, and she said she was.

'It's incredible, right?' he said.

She nodded, telling herself it hadn't been real.

'What did you see?' he asked.

'I don't want to talk about it."

He looked offended. 'Why not?'

'If you want to know, read my mind.'

His shoulders slumped. 'The horseshoe's worn off for me,' he said. 'You took so long getting here.'

'Don't blame me,' she snapped. 'It's not my fault if your drug abuse isn't working out.'

She wished he really could see her thoughts. The whisky and aspirin. Ülle, Jari, and the baby. The green air choking the house.

He wouldn't be able to deal with any of it, but maybe he'd at least stay out of the way.

'Come on,' she said, regaining her feet. 'Let's get you to the centre.'

She'd started toward the road, in her mind already hailing a cab, when she turned to check on him and saw he hadn't moved.

'I can't,' he said. 'Sorry, I can't.'

It was all she could do not to scream. 'Dad, we had a deal!'

'I know. But I can't stay there anymore. I want to go home.'

'I told you, the house is being fumigated.'

'A hotel then.' He sounded hopeful, as if him alone in a hotel room didn't always end in disaster.

She was tempted to say yes. It was the quickest way to get him off her hands. But she'd be breaking a promise she'd made to herself the previous spring, the first time all the colleges had passed her over, the first time she'd wanted to end things. She had sworn that she wouldn't abandon him without first making sure there was someone to look after him.

'When I visited you last week, you were doing so well,' she said. 'You're just afraid to go back because you think they'll be mad about the horseshoe.'

'If you don't want to help me, I'll be fine on my own,' he said.

That was always his attitude. Because of it, her mother had figured she could to go to New Zealand without him. Before she'd left, Regan had asked her why she'd never divorced him, and her mother had smiled a weary smile.

'Honey,' she'd replied, 'you can't ditch somebody just because their life hasn't turned out the way they planned.'

Two weeks later, her mother was sailing across the Pacific.

The wind off the lake picked up and sent the swings in the playground rocking. A bank of black clouds had rolled in from the south, and bands of rain shimmied on the horizon.

'Come on, Dad,' she said, making a decision. 'Let's find a cab.'

'To go where?'

'A hotel, like you said.'

He looked taken aback. 'Well, good.'

They went over to the road. She flagged down a cab, they got in, and she gave the driver the treatment centre's address.

'What are you trying to pull?' her father cried.

'You have to check out.' When he started to protest, she cut him off. 'Don't worry. If they come after you with butterfly nets, I'll body-slam them.'

The cab driver must have been listening, because he asked again where they'd like to go. She could tell that he wanted her father to reply.

'Dad, just tell him the centre,' she said.

In a tone of resignation, he repeated the centre's address. They'd got as far as the Exhibition grounds when he spoke again.

'So you're going to dump me at a hotel and head off to Lucinda?'

'You said you want a hotel room.'

'I want to go home. You're telling me I can't.'

'What am I supposed to do? Ask Lucinda if you can crash at her place?'

'You really want me off your hands, don't you?'

'I told you, it's not up to me. The fumigators – '

'Hey, have you been drinking?'

She clamped her mouth shut. He must have smelled the whisky.

'It's Wednesday afternoon,' he said. 'Why were you drinking on a Wednesday afternoon?'

'Let's consider the irony of you asking that question.'

'Seriously, what's going on? Are you having a rough patch?'

Her father talked of rough patches in the same way that Paul talked of episodes.

'I'm fine,' she said.

'Oh, okay. All right then. No need to be concerned, I guess.'

He said it like that, but then he let it go. At least he was consistent; he'd always claimed that she should be free to make her own mistakes. As a parenting approach, it suited him. The one time they'd tried family counselling, the counsellor had run through the things that her parents weren't supposed to do, like order her to eat, or comment on her appearance, or offer her advice about how to get better, and she'd seen her father's look of relief at hearing he had no responsibilities. But then, as he saw it apparently, he was giving her advice all the time.

She had this thought and had to remind herself that it hadn't been real.

They'd almost reached Bathurst Street when she felt his eyes on her. His pupils were nearly back to normal size.

'I have an idea,' he told her.

'Okay.'

'We should take a vacation.'

'A vacation,' she said.

He gave no sign of sensing her alarm. 'When was the last time we went away together? Years ago, right?'

'Last Christmas. Tampa.'

'Tampa was with Mom. What about the two of us?'

She didn't answer because she didn't know. All through high school, her free time had been eaten up by races and training and injuring herself and trying to get better.

'We'll take a road trip,' he said. 'If we can't be in the house, it's perfect timing.'

'I told you, the car's in the shop.'

'So we rent something.'

'Renting costs too much.'

'God, you're like your mother. What about the money we'll save because I won't be in the centre?'

Then she remembered that she hadn't told him about quitting her job. 'I can't take a vacation,' she said. 'I have to work.'

'Ask the store for time off.'

She said she couldn't. The disappointment on his face was too much, so she turned to stare out the window. It was a relief when he didn't say anything else.

What would happen if she told him about Ülle? Not the whole story; not the part about ordering her. But what if Regan told him that three flatpacks had turned up out of the blue? He might offer to help. He could provide a distraction that would let them sneak off. Or he could come with them, travel in a separate car, sleep in his own tent.

Hunched over beside her, he started to sing, so softly that she couldn't make out the words. The tune wasn't one she knew, but then snatches of it seemed familiar as it shifted between major and minor keys, the notes stretching in a melancholy way.

'What song is that?' she asked.

'Something I wrote at the centre.'

He hadn't written anything for a long time. When she was eight, her mother had told her that her father's career had consisted of raising a daughter but that Regan must never put it like that, not to him or anyone else. She had to say he was a musician. From then on, Regan had thought of him as a kind of undercover agent, so undercover that his true work was a mystery even to himself.

'Will you sing it so I can hear?' she asked him now.

He hardly ever sang his own songs at her request. She had to wait for him to suggest it. The last couple of years, those times had come only when he was high, and pretty much all he sang had been written before she was born.

Now he sat up straight and drew a breath. On the first note, his voice cracked. He glanced at the cab driver, as if to reassure himself that the man wasn't listening, before starting again.

She couldn't follow the words because the tune kept distracting her. It was from a lullaby he'd sung when she was a girl, one that his own father had taught him. She loved its longest, highest note, and then the waxing and waning across the bottom of his range. She remembered a fever in the summer before Grade 1, when boulders the size of battleships had rammed each other in her head. Her father's voice had reached her through the tumult, the song's thin line pulling her back to a world where he held a cool, wet cloth against her forehead.

At that point in her life, things had been simple. You were healthy or sick. You were happy or sad. If something was wrong, your parents fixed it. There were scrapes and bruises but no such thing as injury. There were tears but no depression. Living was just what you did, not something you had to do.

'Dad,' she said. 'Dad, can you stop?'

He broke off. 'Did you notice what I added in there?' he asked.

'Sure. *Child of Each-droim*. It's cool. But listen, will you sing the rest for me later? I've got a bad headache.'

She pressed her temple against the window. Fat drops of rain began to plinko down the glass, merging and splitting like amoebas.

When the cab pulled up at the centre, she got out and paid the driver, but her father stayed sitting in the back seat, arms crossed. It was typical of him to get sulky when he was coming off a high.

'You don't have to go in with me,' she told him, 'but I'm not paying this guy more money to wait.'

Her father stepped out of the cab and followed her inside.

In the lobby, the supervisor was standing behind the reception desk. She put on a good show of welcoming him back, as if his leaving had been an everyday thing, and he made a joke about getting lost on the way to the can.

His room looked the same as it had on Regan's last visit. The self-help books he'd brought still sat on the windowsill. On the rug lay a pair of dumbbells that he'd probably never touched. His guitar was propped up against the dresser. He retrieved his suitcase from the closet and started pulling clothes out of drawers.

'What do you think about staying at the hotel with me?' he said. 'We might get a discount if we take two rooms.'

She could tell he was trying not to sound excited about the idea, like he knew his enthusiasm would be a deal breaker.

'I'm fine at Lucinda's,' she said.

The brightness in his eyes dimmed. 'How am I going to pay for stuff like food?' he said.

'We'll stop for cash. I'll put the room on Mom's credit card.' She waited for him to ask if he could have the card, but he only frowned at the dumbbells. His suitcase was already full, and he hadn't yet packed his books.

'How did I get all this crap here?' he said. 'It'll be a pain in the ass, hauling it to a hotel.'

'So leave the dumbbells.'

'When did you say we can go back in the house?'

'Friday.' It was one more day than she needed, but if she said Thursday, he'd probably claim that the fumigators were being too cautious and that it would be safe to return right away.

He started shoving books into the suitcase, squashing his clothes to make room. Soon he was swearing, pulling out shirts and throwing them to the floor.

'Let me do it,' she said.

He watched while she emptied the suitcase onto the bed and rolled each shirt and pair of pants into a tight cigar before putting it back in. It occurred to her that this might be the last time she ever saw him. She should say something, tell him that it would be all right, that he'd tried his best with her, that he should keep trying with himself.

Half the books were in the suitcase when it became clear that no more were going to fit. They both stared at the case awhile.

'Never mind,' he said. Reaching over, he yanked out a handful of clothes and carried them back to the dresser.

'What are you doing?' she said.

'I changed my mind.' He dropped the clothes into a drawer. 'This place is better than a hotel anyhow. The food's included.'

It was hard to hide her relief. She would have helped him unpack, but she didn't want to seem too gung-ho, so she just sat on the bed until even his toothbrush was back in place. When he'd finished, he took his guitar, sat down beside her, and began to pick out some country tune he'd played a hundred times.

'You know that song you sang in the cab?' she said. 'It's really good, Dad. You should record it.'

He just kept playing, but he began to improvise with little runs and flourishes, showing off for her, before lapsing into chords. 'The last few days, I've been thinking I could do a whole album,' he said. 'With versions of old songs I used to sing for you.'

'That sounds really great.'

'I mean, I wouldn't want to do it unless I could do it right.'

'Well, yeah,' she said.

'Maybe you could sing backup, like you did in middle school. What do you say?'

'That would be amazing.' He couldn't have forgotten that her voice made ears bleed. A lump swelled in her throat. She remembered the playground and the stickiness of the horseshoe on her fingers. 'Dad, you know how you wanted me to read your thoughts? What did you want me to see?'

The guitar fell silent, and his look turned heavy. 'First, tell me what you saw in my head,' he said.

She could imagine no situation in which she'd tell him that. 'There was nothing I didn't already know,' she said.

'Then you didn't see what I wanted you to.'

'Which was what?'

'You'll laugh.'

'I won't, I promise.'

He played that opening bit of Gordon Lightfoot he loved so much, and she knew he was stalling.

'I wanted you to see the album,' he said finally.

He had to be kidding.

'The one you were just talking about?' she said.

'I knew you'd laugh.'

'Dad, I didn't laugh.' But as she said it, she almost did. It was so ridiculous. 'I don't understand. You could have just told me about it.'

'Not the way it's in my head. It's there so perfectly. I'll never be able to record it like it sounds in there.'

She felt her jaw clench. All his wheedling coercion, and for what? So she'd listen to a mental demo tape. The worst thing was, he didn't intend it as a joke. The way he'd spoken, she knew it meant more to him than anything that she should hear what he'd done and approve. Which was strange, given what a disappointment she'd apparently turned out to be.

She stood from the bed.

'Dad, I have to go,' she told him.

He wrapped his arms around the guitar. When she ruffled the top of his hair, he didn't react. She headed for the door.

'Hey, you hear from Michigan yet?' he asked as she reached the threshold.

She told him she hadn't.

'I have a good feeling about Michigan,' he said.

He'd gone to Michigan – for two years anyhow. He liked to brag that he'd made the track team even though he hadn't been on scholarship and hadn't really trained. Regan didn't think a failure to practise was something to brag about.

'Will you visit me tomorrow?' he asked.

'I thought visiting day was Sunday.'

'It is, but I just walked out on them. I'll say I need extra support.'

'Sure,' she said. 'I'll come after work.' He'd be upset when she didn't show up, but things wouldn't go completely haywire until he tried calling her or returning home. Maybe there'd be a way to send word that she was all right.

'Let me walk you to the lobby,' he said.

'No, it's okay.' If he went with her, one of them might have a change of heart. 'Play me out, will you? Play that song from the cab again.'

He started into it so eagerly. She lingered at the door to listen for a few seconds before stepping into the hallway.

Outside, the rain had stopped and every surface glistened. Cars sloshed through puddles, while people carried umbrellas turned useless by the sun. She was ten miles from home. This time last year, she would have run there. Today, the mere thought made her foot ache. Besides, she had no time.

Sitting in another cab, she tried to focus on what was ahead. They'd wait until nightfall, when there weren't as many people out and the darkness would hide them, and then they'd make their way to Lucinda's. With hoodies pulled around Ülle's and Jari's faces, they might pass for normal.

Once the cab reached Regan's neighbourhood, she got the driver to drop her off at the convenience store. From there, she started for the ravine before remembering that the baby needed formula, so she returned to the store, went inside, and scanned the shelves without success. She was about to ask the old man at the counter if they had any baby food when she glanced out through the plate-glass window and noticed a vehicle pulling up. It was the beige van.

Her heart banged against her ribs. She retreated to the back of the store, where there was a door marked Employees Only. She could try it, but if she found no exit on the other side, she'd be trapped, and if the old man saw her, he'd probably raise hell.

The front door chimed and opened. Peeking over the shelves, she saw a thick-set man with a bad comb-over nod to the old guy at the counter and shoot him a grin filled with shark's teeth.

Maybe the goon hadn't spotted her. He might not even know she'd left the house. Or maybe he'd seen her leaving and spent all this time in search of her.

He'd just stopped at the counter when her phone went off. 'Dance of the Sugar Plum Fairy.' Her mother. Of course it was her mother.

She pulled out the phone to kill the ring tone. Footsteps came down the aisle, heavy and unhurried. She pretended to be totally fascinated by what was on the shelves.

The goon stopped and stood beside her. She could hear the low burr of his breathing, and she prayed that he just happened to be interested in Hint of Lime tortilla chips.

'Let's go,' he said quietly. 'Out the front door, nice and easy.'

'Get away from me or I'll scream,' she whispered.

'You don't want to scream. I'd have to hurt you. The old guy at the counter, too.'

'This place has cameras,' she said.

'Let me worry about that,' he replied. 'You know you're not supposed to be out here. We'll get you back in the house, and I won't do anything to you. How's that sound? A free pass. One-time offer.'

She sized up the distance to the Employees Only door. If she got a head start, she might make it.

'There's a problem with the plan you're cooking up right now,' he said. 'You don't know how fast I am and whether I care about the cops. So you've got a choice. Either you leave the store right after I do or you make a fuss and find out some things.'

He grabbed the tortilla chips and took them to the front. She waited until he'd paid before heading out after him.

He was sitting behind the wheel of the van. She got in the passenger side and buckled her seat belt. He started the engine, and she waited to see in which direction he drove, thinking that if he didn't take them toward the house, she'd jump out at a stop sign.

He went in the right direction. As he drove, she snuck glances at his face, his lumpish nose, the hairs sprouting from his ears. He gripped the wheel with the sausagey fingers of a serial strangler.

'So what are you trying to pull?' he said. 'You know the rules.'

'I had to help a family member.'

'Your old man. Yeah, we know about him. Don't give me excuses. You're the one who wanted a flatpack.'

'I only ordered one of them,' she said. 'You sent two more.'

'To help you along. You using an oxygen tank in there?'

'I'm not using anything. Maybe I'm immune.'

'Nobody's immune. Don't go outside again or we'll hurt you. I'm talking seriously here.'

It came to her that if he was that serious, he'd have already hurt her.

'Would you tell me something?' she said. 'Who are they? The flatpacks, I mean.'

He gave a snort. 'None of your business.'

'Are their names Ülle and Jari, maybe?'

The goon stiffened in his seat. 'Where'd you hear those names?'

'She said them. She remembers them.'

'Flatpacks don't remember anything.'

'So those aren't their names?'

He shook his head, whether in denial or a refusal to answer, she couldn't tell.

'You be careful,' he said. 'Curiosity and the cat, right?'

They'd almost reached the cul-de-sac.

'I thought it was illegal to flatpack babies,' she said.

He kept his silence. A minute later, they pulled up at her house. She watched for a twitch of the living room drapes and a glimpse of Ülle.

'Get going,' the goon said. 'From now on, be a good girl.'

'You mean, go back in there and die.'

He grunted in disbelief. 'You break the rules, I don't touch a hair on your head, and you sass me? Fucking teenagers.'

She opened the door and stepped out of the van. 'Thanks for the ride,' she said.

It was only when she found the front door of the house locked that she remembered she didn't have her keys. She thought of knocking, but she wanted to be out of the goon's sightline as soon as possible, so she went around to the back.

The mudroom door was unlocked. Upon opening it, she released a waft of green air into the yard.

'I'm back,' she called out. She was weighing up whether they should stick to their plan when she realized that nobody had responded. She called out again. No reply.

She'd got as far as the hallway when she pulled up short. The air was thick as moss, so that she could barely see the other end. There, outside the bathroom, someone was lying on the floor. She took a few steps forward. It was Paul, and for some reason he was shirtless, and he looked about as dead as she'd once hoped to be by that point in time.

SIX

LETTER TO LITTLE ONE

Little one, I must tell you now about Itzy. Itzy and Jari, Jari and Itzy. Cousins, the youngest of their generation. Jari was the baby of Mormor's clan, without older siblings to protect him from the other children's malice at family gatherings in his youth. It was Itzy who defended him against wrist burns and wet willies, who kept him from being tossed into the sewage pond near Mormor's house. Because Itzy was the second-youngest cousin, his heroics weren't without risk. Perhaps his confidence in performing them came from an apprehension that the other cousins felt uneasy around him, thought him an odd duck. Like Jari, they had overheard the adults in the family whispering about Itzy. The boy didn't lack intelligence. He just had a habit of staying silent when you expected him to speak, and then, when you expected him to stay silent, of saying the most awful things. Mormor seemed merely to tolerate the rest of her grandchildren, as one tolerates television commercials and days of high humidity. Itzy was the sole child she flagrantly adored.

When Mormor left for the Americas with Jari and Ülle, Itzy stayed behind to oversee the flatpacking factory. His principal task was to keep track of the money, but he liked to spend time on the factory floor, testing equipment, tinkering with it, even cleaning up the place. Everyone else there wore masks because of the fumes, but Itzy went bare-headed, convinced that inhaling the flatpacking chemicals would grant him an immunity to the worm. Though others mocked the idea, he kept on living while others died. He boasted that he could run the factory single-handed, and he didn't heed Mormor when, after hearing of his penchant for mopping the floors, she said it wasn't right for a member of her family to act like a janitor. Jari claimed that Itzy was the only person he knew who could get away with disobeying Mormor.

In the old country, Ülle had met Itzy a few times at family gatherings, most of them while she was still a nanny. Although he was Jari's elder, he looked and sounded younger, speaking in a chirrupy staccato without a single line wizening his face. He'd taken an interest in her from the start, repeatedly asking her whether she needed a break from minding Jari's daughter, whether she wanted some cider, whether she'd found a boyfriend. He seemed always to enter her vicinity just when she was looking around with the hope of glimpsing Mormor, who, as it turned out, never attended such get-togethers – part of her habit of carefulness.

After becoming Jari's lover, Ülle attended only two more family events, both funerals. Both times, Jari and Itzy ended the day drunk, with Itzy leering at Ülle and praising Jari for moving on. Both times, Jari said the next morning that he worried about Itzy, that his cousin had always been a queer one, but that he'd changed since working at the factory. Once, he'd been demure at large gatherings. Now his voice was the loudest in the room.

When they arrived in the Americas, there was so little talk of what they'd left behind that Ülle gave no thought to Itzy beyond feeling glad that he hadn't joined them. She didn't know why he'd stayed, but she assumed that it was to oversee the factory. Little one, you'll find it's often true that when you don't much like someone, and when they aren't physically present in your life, you're happy to go along with other people's failure to mention them.

Then, one morning two weeks after Ülle's appointment with Dr. Ramachandran, Jari told her to set an extra place for dinner, because Itzy was coming to live with them.

Jari's excitement in sharing the news was partial compensation for the news itself. The past two weeks, almost nothing had been said between him and Ülle. There'd been no talk of the doctor's whereabouts or of Jari's diagnosis. He and Ülle both knew what was coming, and they were too frightened to speak of it. Each night, he returned home later than the last. At dinners, he and Mormor wolfed their food, then cloistered themselves for hours in Mormor's office. Whatever they discussed in there, he never told Ülle. Each morning, he looked a little gaunter. Dark rings thickened, day by day, around his eyes. His skin gained the odour of turpentine. When Ülle asked about it, he said it was from a tincture he'd been prescribed.

You saw another doctor? she asked.

A homeopathist, he said.

She remembered all the folk remedies for the worm that people in the old country had tried. Garlic enemas, mustard poultices, gizzard tea. Nothing worked.

While Jari wasted away, things in Mormor's office changed. Heavy weights could be heard thundering to the floor every day. According to Jari, Mormor had abandoned her strength training years ago, after a doctor's warning about her heart. Now she was convinced that the decline in her physical powers had brought about a weakening of her brain – one that could be reversed if she returned her attention to her body.

Jari didn't like her lifting weights. The exercise would trigger imbalances in her acid levels, no two ways about it. But she couldn't be dissuaded, so Ülle went about dreading the thud of medicine balls, the clang of dumbbells. There was no predicting when the noise would start or how long it would last.

Little one, you may wonder how Ülle managed at such a time. It's true that if she'd been plunged into her life in Tkaronto directly from her life before the worm, she might have struggled to preserve her sanity. But by the time she'd reached the Americas, she no longer thought of pain and privation as impediments to life; for a long time, they had been her life's conditions.

When Jari announced that Itzy would be joining them, he seemed so pleased that Ülle couldn't help feeling pleased, too.

But as he went on to tell her that he and Itzy would be embarking on a new business venture, something Jari wasn't at liberty to discuss, there was a wildness in his eyes that unsettled her. She wondered if the news about Itzy meant that the flatpacking factory had shut down. In Tkaronto, the authorities must have executed their duties with care because, since the day of Cata the professor's abduction, she'd seen no other flatpacked people on the street.

She spent the day preparing for Itzy's arrival. The casserole had just gone in the oven when she heard the front door open and a familiar high-pitched voice called out Mormor's name. In reply came the eager thump of Mormor's footsteps down the stairs. By the time Ülle had made her way to the foyer, Itzy was already joking with Jari and Mormor about the blue-and-purple cap on his head. Jari said that it must have set off alarms at Oyster Island, and Itzy said no, he'd worn it only at night during the crossing, asleep in his berth and dreaming of his dear Mormor. This remark sent Mormor into fits of laughter.

When Itzy saw Ülle approaching, he spread his arms.

Angel! he said. What a beauty you are! He gave her a wet kiss on each cheek.

Itzy, introduce Ülle to your little fellow, said Mormor.

In Ülle's focus on Itzy, she hadn't noticed the plastic carrier at his feet. Strapped into it was a baby, perhaps three or four months old. A shock of red hair spiked from its head, and it wore a fuzzy myrtle jumper that looked two sizes too big.

Ah yes, said Itzy. He crouched and lifted the baby to his chest. This bounder, he said, is my son.

I didn't know you had a child, said Ülle, feeling a sudden unease.

It was a surprise to me, too, he said with a laugh.

What's his name? said Ülle.

He doesn't have one, Itzy replied. Seeing her look of confusion, he grinned. He had a name when I inherited him, Itzy went on, but it's such an abomination that I refuse to pronounce it. I'm waiting for a new one to come to me.

Have you ever heard such a thing? said Mormor with a chuckle.

At dinner, while the child slept in the carrier, Itzy told them the story. The baby had been brought to him only a few weeks previous, after the mother died of the worm. Up until the moment the child's grandparents arrived on Itzy's doorstep, he hadn't known there was a child, nor had he been aware of the mother's illness.

It was just a fling, he said. A single night, and then I never heard from her again. Apparently, she waited for her deathbed to tell her parents about me. Of course, I was ready to deny everything, but he's the spitting image, isn't he?

Although Itzy addressed these remarks to the whole table, Ülle suspected that she was the only one who hadn't previously heard them, because Mormor just smiled and nodded, while Jari ate like he wasn't listening. Itzy explained that the baby had been the reason for his emigration, that he'd felt obliged to take custody, but he knew nothing about caring for an infant.

In any case, he said, I've saved the little beggar's life by importing him. You'll know what to do from here on in.

He spoke these words directly to Ülle.

Her eyes darted to Mormor, then to Jari. Mormor reached for the butter. Jari stared at his plate. Everything had been decided then. No wonder Jari hadn't mentioned the baby.

Usually, he helped her with clearing up after dinner, but that night it was left to her alone, while Mormor dandled the baby in the dining room and her grandsons looked on. Ülle could hear them jovially cautioning Mormor not to forget her strength and crush the boy. Only once Ülle had finished the dishes and rejoined them did they discuss arrangements for the baby's care. Itzy announced that he'd look after the first night's feedings, saying it as though his munificence was to be admired. When Ülle pointed out that they didn't have supplies, Jari responded that Driver had acquired the essentials. Then Jari and Itzy went upstairs to assemble the crib Driver had bought, while Mormor handed the child to Ülle and disappeared into her office.

That night in bed, Jari spoke before Ülle did.

I'm sorry about the baby, he said. We'll find someone to help you. Itzy and I just need to take care of some business first.

What is this business? she demanded.

I told you before, he replied. I can't say anything.

The next morning, he made a show of feeding the baby breakfast. The baby fussed and refused his bottle, until Jari grew irritated and said he had to leave. Eventually, Ülle left, too, along with Driver and the baby, carrying a list of provisions. In the stores, Driver lugged bags and baskets while Ülle carried the baby, who whimpered and screamed by turns. People shot them spiteful looks, and Ülle worried that they mistook her and Driver for the child's parents. Driver told the baby to shut up, and Ülle asked what he hoped to achieve by saying such a thing. When he suggested that they go home, Ülle said there were supplies they needed now, not later, and it wasn't her fault that she'd been put in such an impossible position.

As if to punish her for these words, a stink rose from the baby. They looked in vain for a bathroom with a changing table. When Ülle said she'd change the baby on the floor, Driver insisted that Mormor would never permit it, and in the end they drove home with the child wailing and the car awash in the smell of its dung.

From then on, Ülle spent her days in a social circle consisting of herself, the baby, and Driver. Jari and Itzy continued to leave the house first thing each day, while Mormor's presence consisted of little more than the thump of weights. The baby cried for hours, his excrement a brown broth that leaked from his diaper, and soon he refused to sleep unless lying on Ülle's chest. She didn't know how her body had become such necessary furniture to someone who'd only just encountered it. All the time he dozed against her, she could do nothing except hold him.

Ensnared in such wakefulness, she learned the house's nocturnal habits. She became familiar with the two times each night, once at one thirty and then again at four forty-five, when Mormor visited the bathroom. She learned that on Wednesday nights, Driver entered Mormor's bedchamber at eleven fifteen and left at twelve fifteen. Once, Ülle met him in the hallway as he was emerging. They locked eyes for a moment and didn't speak.

Infant shit, failed feedings, sleepless nights. She'd been through this life before. It hadn't been easier the first time, but her situation then had been of her own making, which had rendered the child easier to love. Now, even on the few occasions when Itzy's baby smiled at her, she felt no fondness, only a base satisfaction at her performance of a duty. She didn't know if she would ever grow to feel differently. The baby wasn't like you, little one. She knew he felt no fondness for her either. At that age, he wouldn't even regard her as a separate being.

Ülle and Jari barely saw each other anymore, except the nights she stayed up with him and Itzy while they drank and reminisced about their childhood. Those times, Jari seemed indifferent to her. One night, he began to speak with great sadness about his wife.

That sweet woman, he said. Dying with our daughter, and where was I? Out following Mormor's orders.

It couldn't be helped, said Itzy, slurring his words. It was for the family.

The family! said Jari. Mormor's family, not mine.

Stop it, said Itzy. You mustn't say such things.

Tears spilled from Jari's eyes. The smell of turpentine was overwhelming. Ülle wanted to put her arms around him, but she feared what it would mean if he refused her touch, so she just sat there watching the baby on the floor in front of her while the child burbled and kicked his little feet.

The baby's room was next to the one she shared with Jari. Even those rare nights when the child accepted his place in the crib, Ülle was obliged to go to him three or four times to soothe and feed him.

You're a good mother, Jari said once after she returned to bed.

I'm not his mother, she replied.

You are in the ways that matter, he said. Treat him as yours, and he'll come to feel like yours.

Like ours, you mean, she said.

He didn't acknowledge her correction.

In the evenings after dinner, when the baby's appetite was sated and his mood agreeable, Mormor rocked and sang to him while Itzy hung about, injecting himself into the proceedings as much as possible, though seldom to the point of holding the baby. Those times he did, he kept the child at arm's length, as one would hold a kitten destined for a sack at the river bottom. During these sessions, Jari always contrived to be elsewhere, while Ülle lingered in the room as per Mormor's expectations, waiting for the inevitable moment when the baby cried and Itzy or Mormor handed him to her.

There was no further mention of a child for Ülle and Jari. Now, the only times Mormor spoke to Ülle were about how to look after Itzy's baby. She had very precise ideas. There must be diaper changes every three hours, whether or not the baby needed them. If he had a cough, Ülle should boil a bottle of ginger ale down to a syrup, then let it cool before dosing him. When first greeting him in the mornings, because it was important to socialize him but also to avoid passing on germs before his immune system could handle them, Ülle was not to kiss him but to shake his hand. At bath times, she must salt the water to toughen his skin. And she was never to let him suck his thumb, lest he become a chronic masturbator like his great-uncle Gunnar.

Mormor and Jari's after-dinner confabulations in her office had ended. At meals, the two of them hardly acknowledged each other. Mormor's attention was all on the baby, while Jari seemed to recede deep within himself. One night in bed, feeling bold,

Ülle asked him whether something had come between him and his grandmother. He said he didn't know what she meant.

Does she still blame you for the doctor's disappearance? Ülle asked.

The doctor is all in the past, he replied.

Have you told Mormor about being tested? said Ülle. Upon asking the question, she held her breath, in doubt of her own daring; he'd never explicitly acknowledged the test to Ülle herself.

Of course, he said. I tell Mormor everything.

The next evening, after the baby had fallen asleep and Ülle was alone washing dishes, Itzy entered the kitchen. He sat down at the table and went about watching her, saying nothing.

Where's Jari? she asked.

I have no idea, Itzy said, without the slightest lapse in his staring.

To break the silence, she spoke the first words that came to her mind.

The baby throws such tantrums, she said. How did you manage to keep him quiet during the sea crossing?

He laughed as if he found the question entertaining.

The key thing, he said, is not to let a baby put you at its beck and call. You must go to it only when it suits you. On the ship, whenever the bambino cried, I left him in the cabin and took a stroll on deck. Every time, I returned to tranquility, and those times I didn't, I went for a second stroll, even a third. It always worked.

He said that he couldn't see why women coddled their children, enslaving themselves to creatures barely out of the pupal phase. If men had been put in charge of parenting from the start, a system such as his would have been universalized long ago.

Yes, it's a shame, said Ülle. If only women allowed men to be more involved.

Itzy gave her a sidelong look.

You're a pert one! he said. Another girl in your position wouldn't be so brave.

Hearing the edge in his voice, she chastised herself. Itzy was just the type to repeat her words to Mormor.

He must have understood the expression on her face, because he laughed again.

Oh, I'm not offended, he said. I admire your cheek! It goes well with your looks.

She asked him again where Jari was.

Where's Jari, where's Jari, he said. You know, I'm afraid that you mustn't come to depend too much on the poor fellow.

The words stole her breath. Itzy knew. How dare he speak of it? She hated him more than she'd ever hated anybody.

These days, he said, one must cultivate friendships widely. You never know whose help you might need.

She was sure that if she remained in the room any longer, she'd shout at him.

I should check on the baby, she said.

To leave, she had to pass by the table. Her skin prickled with the presentiment that he would reach out to touch her. Sure enough, she felt his fingers graze her elbow. When she smacked them away without breaking stride, he laughed hysterically.

Off to the pipsqueak! he called as she mounted the stairs. The little tyrant!

The baby was still sleeping in his crib. Ülle sat nearby in the rocking chair for some time, thinking it ironic that the room was the one least likely for Itzy to enter.

By the time she joined Jari in bed that night, she'd made up her mind to recount what had happened. It didn't matter that Itzy was Mormor's pet. Together, she and Jari would decide what to do.

When she turned to him, though, her attention was caught by a lustre on his face.

You're sweating, she said. Are you all right?

Just trying a new cleansing medicine, he replied.

She pressed her palm to his forehead and felt an appalling heat.

You're burning up, she exclaimed.

An effect of the purgation, he said.

The hardness in his voice stopped her from saying more. She switched off the bedside lamp and tried to sleep, but her mind returned to Itzy in the kitchen, and her determination to speak of him surged. Staring into blackness, she told Jari that she worried about his cousin.

Jari asked her what she meant.

It's the way he talks to me, she said. Always teasing, insinuating.

That's how he is with everyone, Jari replied.

And tonight in the kitchen, he touched me, she said.

He touched you? said Jari.

On my elbow as I walked past, she said.

Your elbow, he said.

Don't say it like that, she cried. I don't want to be left alone with him anymore.

The darkness was unbearable. Turning on the lamp, she readied herself to insist that Jari do something. When she looked at him, she let out a cry of surprise. His brow was covered in blood.

With a frown, he wiped his forehead, then stared at the redness slicking his fingers. A bloody sheen coated his shoulders, too. She pulled back the blanket covering the two of them and saw that it was stained crimson for the length of his body. At the sight, he scrambled from the bed, dragging the blanket with him and exposing a bloody imprint on the mattress where he'd lain.

Where's it coming from? she said.

His face had gone pale. Blood dribbled down behind his ears.

I'm sweating it, he said. It's fine. I was told it might happen.

We have to get you to a hospital, she said. You could be poisoned.

He gave a shaky laugh.

I do think it's a poison, he said. But I'm not the one it's meant to kill.

Jari, please, she said.

Really, I'm all right, he replied. I'll sit in the bathtub and let it run its course.

He didn't sound as composed as he wished to appear. After starting out of the room with the blanket wrapped around him, he turned in the doorway.

I'm sorry, he said. I didn't mean to ruin the bed.

It's not the bed that matters, she replied.

With the blanket, he wiped at his face and arms.

I'm doing everything I can to live, he said. So nobody can say I didn't try.

Then he headed down the hallway.

She followed him to the bathroom and sat on the white-tiled floor while he lay in an empty tub slowly filling with his blood. He started to moan, and she said it might help to bathe in cold water. He complained as the water rose and pinked around him, saying he'd end up dying of hypothermia, but after a few minutes the bloody sweating ended. They returned to the bedroom and changed the sheets, and he kissed her on the forehead and said that the cold water had been a good idea.

The next day, after he and Itzy had departed and the baby was sleeping off his breakfast, she went to Mormor's office. From within came the sound of clanging weights. Ülle had never knocked on Mormor's door without a summons, and she didn't want to interrupt a workout, but she thought it better than barging in on whatever else Mormor did in there. She tapped softly, then harder. She was about to give up when the clanging stopped and Mormor's voice barked at her to come inside.

The office had the reek of a gymnasium. Old rubber, body odour, antiseptic spray. Blue mats hid the floor. Against the wall sat a metal rack full of dumbbells. In front of it lay three medicine balls, dark brown, like colossal chocolates. On the facing wall stretched a floor-to-ceiling mirror in four panels. Ülle had no idea when any of these things had been installed.

Mormor stood in the middle of the room wearing a liver-coloured track suit darkened by pockets of sweat. A thick leather belt girded her waist. In her hands she held a strange contraption, a fourfold line of metal springs with a handle binding them at either end, and she was stretching them across her chest, then letting them snap back together, repeating this motion over and over while the device creaked like the bed of a honeymooning couple.

Ülle would have thought it impossible for Mormor to get much bigger, but she appeared more swollen than ever. Judging by her skin's yellowish tinge and the tumescence of the veins in her neck, a muscle attack was imminent. She kept on working the contraption, each time stretching the springs further, before tossing it to the floor.

I look better now, don't I? she said, reaching for a towel. For years, I told myself that what mattered were brains. That in this world, brute force isn't what wins.

She ran the towel across her neck, then slid it up under her top to wipe her belly.

If the worm comes for me, I'll give it a fight, she said.

Going over to her desk, she retrieved a syringe and a purple vial.

No need for your help this time, she said. After rolling up a sleeve, she filled the syringe and sunk the needle into her arm. Even across the room, Ülle could hear the hiss. Mormor's countenance became serene, and it seemed the right moment for Ülle to speak.

I'd like to talk about Jari's diagnosis, she said.

Mormor pulled out the needle and returned the syringe to the desk.

I want to ask, Ülle went on, if you'll consider him being flatpacked.

Mormor wheeled on her, and Ülle hurried to get out what she meant to say.

If he's flatpacked, she said, there's a chance that one day they'll be able to restore his memory –

The flatpacks are toxic, Mormor growled. The factory is closed.

He told me that unofficially it's still open, Ülle said.

Did he also tell you that he wants to be flatpacked? said Mormor.

When Ülle didn't reply, Mormor went to the rack of dumbbells and snatched up the two biggest. She began to curl them in front of herself, her biceps flexing without apparent strain.

I wouldn't be surprised if he did want it, Mormor said. He's always been weak.

The shock of the words broke Ülle out of her silence.

That isn't true, she said.

He was weak with that doctor, said Mormor, breathing harder. It was sentimental foolishness, doing what he did. Before that, he was weak with his wife and girl.

What do you mean? said Ülle.

He did what you're doing, said Mormor. Tried to convince me that they should be flatpacked.

Seeing the bewilderment on Ülle's face, Mormor gained a self-satisfied expression and returned the dumbbells to the rack.

Didn't tell you that, did he? she said. Has he told you that his wife insisted on not being flatpacked? He went behind her back, asking me. He can't stand the idea of anybody suffering. That's what I mean by weakness.

But now he's the one suffering, said Ülle. It's no weakness to want to save him.

Flatpacking doesn't save you, said Mormor. She retreated to the window, drew the curtains back, and peered into the night.

Have you ever lived with a flatpack? she asked.

Ülle replied that she hadn't.

Has Jari told you about his aunt Greta? Mormor said.

When Ülle said no, Mormor told her she wasn't surprised.

Greta was the third of my children with the worm, she said. Thorben, then Vauthog, then her. Flatpacking wasn't possible for the boys. It came just after Greta's diagnosis. I remember how excited she was. It sounded like a miracle. At that point, the Church hadn't taken a stand. I agreed to let her go through with it.

Mormor reached out to tug the curtains closed again.

What they sent back wasn't Greta, she said. She didn't recognize us. She couldn't speak. She drooled and messed herself. If no one was around to stop her, she ate from the dog's bowl. For two months, we did our best with her. Then she went into a home.

I'm sorry, said Ülle. I know it doesn't change things, but later on, they improved the process –

You think I don't know? Mormor snapped. They're still animals. Still eating off the floor. You want to see Jari do that?

Of course not, said Ülle. But –

Then don't bother me with fantasies, said Mormor.

She went to her desk, picked up a file folder, and opened it as though to read the contents. It was Ülle's signal to leave, but she didn't move.

Do you know what Jari's been doing? Ülle asked. What he's been taking to keep himself alive for his grandmother? Last night, he was sweating blood.

Mormor's features remained impassive.

You know how it will be once the worm seizes him, said Ülle. Much worse than blood.

Mormor gave a curt nod, but her eyes stayed fixed on the folder. After waiting in vain for a response, Ülle showed herself to the door.

The next two days at dinner, Mormor and Jari barely spoke. Ülle occupied herself with bussing things from the kitchen to the dining room and back. Itzy filled the time with chatter, and when he wasn't chattering, he stared at her brazenly. If Mormor noticed him doing it, she said nothing, while Jari seemed always to be looking the other way. Ülle decided to take matters into her own hands. The next time Itzy's eyes rested on her, she asked him if something was wrong for him to gawk like that. He laughed and denied looking in her direction, but he didn't do it again.

Early the following afternoon, while Ülle was cleaning up from lunch, Itzy returned home unexpectedly.

You're looking very beautiful today, he told her as he walked into the kitchen.

She asked what he was doing home.

I've come to fetch you, he said. Jari has told me to take you to the place where he and I are working.

Why? she demanded.

Am I my cousin's keeper? he replied. Come and find out for yourself.

What about the baby? she said.

Itzy shot her a dirty look that suggested he hadn't considered the baby.

Leave him with Driver, he said.

Driver's out with Mormor, she replied.

Then you'll have to bring the little grub, Itzy said.

His van lacked a car seat, but he insisted that they be on their way, so Ülle clasped the baby tightly while Itzy drove them over the great viaduct across the Wonscotonach Valley to the east side of the city. He swerved from lane to lane and braked hard at stoplights, slamming his foot on the accelerator the moment they turned green. It seemed certain that the baby would start to cry, but he stayed fast asleep in her arms. She said that she was going to be sick and needed to get out.

Calm down, Itzy replied. We'll be there in two shakes.

Ten minutes passed before they pulled into a parking lot filled with potholes and came to a stop beside a brown brick warehouse taking up half the block. It had tall, narrow windows that were blacked out at the bottom.

After exiting the van, Itzy walked around to the passenger-side window. In one hand, he held a plastic water bottle. With the other, he offered her a yellow capsule.

For the nausea, he said.

She hesitated, then thanked him and plucked it from his palm.

Itzy led them to the warehouse door. Inside, the air was clammy. Giant fan blades turned at a decrepit pace above their heads, and long, venous cracks ran across the concrete floor.

Where's Jari? Ülle asked. I don't want the baby in such a place.

Come, said Itzy. They crossed to a door that opened into a smaller chamber with white walls and fluorescent lighting. Reluctantly, she followed him inside.

The room held steel tables laden with computers and laboratory implements, as well as several large machines with unimaginable uses. In the centre of the space sat a great silver vat filled with green liquid that looked thick as a milkshake.

Where's Jari? Ülle asked again.

He's coming, Itzy said. He gestured for her to sit in a folding chair beside one of the tables. Her instinct was to decline, but the baby had grown heavy in her arms. She sat and surveyed the room more closely. For the first time, she noticed the stack of rolled-up carpets encased in plastic along one wall. Except they weren't carpets. When she realized what they were, she bolted from the chair.

Sit, sit, Itzy told her with a laugh. They're sealed, they can't hurt anybody.

Did you flatpack them? she asked. You and Jari?

No, they're from overseas, he replied. An acquaintance squirrelled them away before they could be destroyed.

Why do you have them? she demanded.

You're so curious! he said. Would you believe there are buyers for them? Collectors of curiosities, and a few who want to die but are too cowardly to do it alone in the usual ways. You won't hear it on the news, but death by flatpack is quite gratifying. The toxins give you all these wonderful sensations. Ha! That's humanity for you. Always finding off-label uses.

He seemed to marvel at the thought before turning to her with a look of concern.

How do you feel? he said. Is the pill working? Are you over your carsickness?

He retrieved a plastic tub from a closet and lined it with a towel.

Put the baby in here, he said. That way, I can show you everything while we wait.

There seemed no good reason to argue, so she lowered the sleeping baby into the tub, which Itzy set on the table beside her, just out of reach.

You're making flatpacks, aren't you? she said. If you haven't yet, you're going to.

Such a bright girl, he replied.

But who is there to flatpack? she said. Nobody in this country has the worm.

As soon as she said it, she realized the answer.

This was Jari and Itzy's furtive mission then. Perhaps it was the real reason Itzy had come to Tkaronto. She couldn't bring herself to raise the possibility aloud, because she didn't want to talk about it with Itzy. She hated the idea of him rubbing it in her face that Jari's secret had been kept from her and shared with him. Jari must not have told Mormor either or she'd have spoken differently in her office.

Itzy went to the vat of green liquid and slowly circled it, babbling out an answer about their prospective clientele. He explained that some people weren't right in the head, that they'd be happy to be flatpacked even without the worm. If you were of a certain frame of mind, flatpacking had great appeal. As long as you weren't unsealed, you'd stay forever just as you'd been, and maybe one day the technology would allow someone to inflate you, fix your body, fix your brain, whatever was wrong with you, whatever made you prefer being flatpacked to living your life.

Ülle looked around the room.

You built all this? she asked.

Oh no, he replied. Most of it's from the old country. The border's closed only to people, not to things.

Then he came over to her, once more wearing a solicitous expression.

Is the pill helping yet? he said. You're such a pretty girl, it's a shame for you to feel ill.

He put a hand on her shoulder.

I'm fine, she said, trying not to let her panic reach her voice. She wanted to push his hand off, but that would do away with all pretence, and pretence might yet be useful. It might allow her an escape.

I'm worried about Jari, she said. We should call to see what's happened to him.

No, no, we mustn't do that, Itzy said. You're really feeling better now?

He sighed as if resigning himself to something. Then he withdrew his hand.

I must make a confession, he said. I didn't bring you here because Jari asked me to.

She got up and moved to retrieve the baby, but Itzy blocked her way.

Sit, he told her. You mustn't act like a girl left alone with a dirty old man. The truth is, I wanted to talk with you about Jari.

Ülle didn't sit.

What about him? she asked.

Have you not figured it out? Itzy said. My dear, your mind's been taken up too much by that tadpole over there. Look at this place. I brought you here to show you what's on the brink of happening.

She felt a wave of revulsion, and not only because it was Itzy telling her the news. The day before, she'd lobbied Mormor for just this outcome, yet now it seemed a terrible mistake. Perhaps learning of Greta had affected her in ways she hadn't realized. It wasn't that she wanted Jari to go compliantly to his death. But what if he were flatpacked and they never found a way to restore his memories? What if, right after the procedure, they found a cure for the worm?

It seemed that Itzy was pondering similar questions.

You have to remember that someone who's flatpacked can't expect to be awakened right away, he said. Not until we solve the off-gassing problem. So, my dear, you must steel yourself. Who knows how long you'll be without your beloved.

He uttered the epithet with naked scorn, and she knew for certain that he hadn't brought her here to tell her anything.

Itzy, you must take us home, she said.

He drew a breath that he held until his face went scarlet.

Why does a girl like you choose a fellow like Jari? he said. Is it simply looks? Because he isn't a handsome man, I must say.

Ülle moved again for the baby, and this time Itzy let her take the child from the tub.

Or is it something else that attracts you? he continued. Jari's advantages, shall we say? You were lucky to start going with a man of our family when you did. Is that how a girl like you operates? You needn't deny it, I'll still respect you. I might respect you more!

Take us home, she said. I need to feed the baby.

The baby, he scoffed. Always the baby!

Itzy reached to snatch him from her. Instinctively, she held on tighter, until she realized that Itzy was pulling at the child's arm without compunction. The baby screamed. She handed him over and watched Itzy rock him with a theatrical show of care.

Give him back, she said. You've hurt him.

Ignoring her, Itzy began to sing. The melody was from an old lullaby, but the words he sang were *Shut up, shut up, you nasty little shrimp.*

Itzy, please, said Ülle.

You see how unfair my life is, he said. Even my own son rejects me. I'd have left him in the old country if I hadn't told Mormor about him. I swear, I should put him out of his misery.

He carried the baby to the vat and mimed heaving him over the side.

Stop it! cried Ülle. She inched toward them, not daring to get too close.

It would be a kindness to you, Itzy told her. Do you think that with this turnip around, Mormor will let you be anything more than a nursemaid?

The baby kept up his wailing. Ülle was preparing to rush forward when Itzy broke into a grin.

You don't know how to take a joke, do you? he said. Here, put a stop to all this blubbering.

He handed the baby to her, and they returned to the van. By the time they'd reached the house, the baby had quieted and Ülle had decided what she would say to Itzy. When they pulled into the driveway, though, he was the one who spoke first. There was a cool detachment in his voice she'd never heard before.

You mustn't breathe a word about our trip, he said. If you tell anyone, I'll say that you tricked me into thinking Jari wanted me to drive you there. It's not my wish, but if you start casting aspersions, I'll have no choice. You understand, don't you?

She said that she did. It was only once she was back in the house and the baby lay safely in his crib, only once Mormor would hear her if she screamed, that she sought out Itzy in the living room, where he sat watching television.

Itzy, I must ask something of you, she said. You must promise to tell me when you're about to flatpack Jari.

I don't know what you mean, he said with a wink.

Be quiet, she said. I don't want to hear anything more from you except your promise. Swear that you'll tell me before the day arrives, and in return, I promise not to tell Mormor about the pill you tried to give me.

Tried? he said.

She swept her fist out from behind her back, opening it to reveal the pill before closing it again and jamming it into her pocket.

Itzy's eyes filled with craziness. He looked on the brink of hurling himself at her. Then Mormor's footsteps creaked overhead, and he sunk back into the couch.

Oh, Ülle, he said with a sudden smile. I told you before, the pill was to help with your nausea. It's quite harmless. Give it to me, I'll take it myself, you'll see.

She ignored his request.

Promise, she said. Promise to tell me before anything happens.

His smile fell away.

Yes, yes, all right, he muttered.

He got up and stalked from the room. A minute later, there was the sound of the van starting and driving away.

She spent the rest of the day anticipating a talk with Jari. That evening, he and Itzy didn't return home until after dinner. When they did, Itzy went straight upstairs to Mormor's office. No doubt he'd readied some lie to inoculate himself against Ülle's accusations. Ülle let him go. She'd thought of speaking to Mormor first, but it didn't seem worth the risk. Even if Mormor believed her, she might take Itzy's side.

Once Ülle and Jari were alone together in their room, she told him what had happened, explaining about the pill, not mentioning the location because she didn't want to confuse the matter.

When she finished, Jari didn't respond at first.

It was a misunderstanding, he said finally.

She felt the air go from her.

It must have been just a stomach pill, he said.

It wasn't, she exclaimed. I'll show you – I'll take it.

She went to the bureau that held her clothes. As soon as she pulled open the top drawer, she knew that someone had gone through it. The socks in which she'd hidden the pill lay at the bottom, but the pill was gone.

He's stolen it, she said. Her whole body began to shake.

Jari came over to hold her.

We'll fix things, he said. I'll talk with him. I won't stand for the two of you fighting.

It wasn't a fight, she cried. Didn't you hear what I said?

There's been a misunderstanding, he repeated.

Something's wrong with him, she insisted. You've said it yourself.

But he's still Itzy, he said. You don't know him like I do.

She threw herself onto the bed and lay with her face buried in a pillow. When she looked up after a few minutes, he'd left the room.

Next door, the baby was crying. She hated the baby. She hated that he didn't have a name. She hated that he stirred in her not even a hint of parental love. After she coaxed him back to sleep, she returned to bed and dreamed that her parents were alive again. When she awoke, the sun was out and an eerie silence filled her ears. Jari was still absent from the room. It was seven thirty, long after the baby's usual breakfast time. She went to his crib, and he wasn't there.

Searching the house, she found no sign of anyone. The van and limousine were missing. She knocked on the door of Mormor's office and got no response. She tried to open it and discovered it was locked.

Only when she returned to her and Jari's room to dress did she see the sheet of paper folded in half and lying on his pillow. The words written on it were in his childish hand.

I've gone to do to myself what I couldn't for my wife and child. I'm sorry for not telling you. I didn't want you having to keep a secret from Mormor. Now she'll learn of things soon enough.

Be good to Itzy's boy. You're sweet and lovely – better than I deserved. One day, they'll solve the off-gassing and we'll be reunited. If I return not knowing myself, I hope you will take care of me. For now, I've made Mormor promise to protect you.

Ülle ran to her laptop and searched for the name of a cab company. Five minutes later, she was waiting in front of the house by the wrought-iron fence that encircled the property. Five minutes after that, she was sitting in the back of a taxi on her way to the warehouse.

SEVEN
COLLABORATOR

Regan hurried to where Paul lay at the end of the hallway and knelt next to him. A red gash split his forehead. The blood had run down his face and spilled onto the carpet.

'Paul,' she said. 'Paul Stevens!' As if speaking his full name was the key to his revival.

She felt for his pulse. It bopped on her finger, brisk and even, like a drummer unaware that the rest of the band had fled the stage.

'Regan,' he murmured. Then his eyes popped open, wide and wild. 'Flatpacks,' he shouted.

'Don't get up. It's okay, they're gone.' Whether or not it was true, it seemed like the best thing to say.

'They're in the bathroom.' His hand went to his forehead. 'No, they got out. She hit me with – I can't remember.'

'Don't touch it. You need a doctor.'

'I thought you were here,' he said. 'I was saving you.'

Farther along the hallway, at the edge of the kitchen, something lay on the floor. A steak knife, covered not in Paul's blood but in what looked like green paint. The floor and walls were streaked with the same bright shade. The sight flooded her with horror.

'Did you hurt them?' she exclaimed.

'They tried to kill me.' He said it in a plaintive way, like a little kid insisting that his brother had started it.

'What did you do to them?'

'I don't remember.'

'There was a baby. What about the baby?'

'Baby?' He nodded slowly. 'Right, the baby.' Sitting up, he turned toward the kitchen. 'It's okay. I stopped it.'

She got to her feet. 'What do you mean?'

'The off-gassing,' he said. 'I didn't hurt it. I just sealed it up.'

'In what? You can't seal them up!' She ran to the kitchen.

'So I could deal with the other two,' she heard him say.

A white trash bag sat on the counter. It had been tied shut with a clumsy knot, but someone had ripped it open. When she parted the sides of the tear to reach in, there was nothing there.

She went through the house from top to bottom, shouting Ülle's and Jari's names. She checked the closets and cupboards, under the beds. In her parents' room, she snuck a glance out through the blinds and saw the beige van parked in the cul-de-sac. Returning to Paul, she found him trying to stand.

'Stay lying down,' she said. 'I'm calling 911.' It would bring the cops and send the dealer's goon into a rage, but she couldn't think of a better option. It didn't matter anyway. Paul would never agree to keep quiet about this.

When she pulled out her phone, she saw there'd been a text from Lucinda. All it said was '*HMMMM.*'

Ülle and Jari had gone there with the baby. It was the only thing that made sense. Ülle must have explained to Lucinda about the dealer, so she was being careful in what she wrote.

Regan called 911. She told them there was somebody with a head injury in the backyard. Then she hung up, helped Paul to his feet, and walked him down the hallway to the mudroom door. As they reached the lawn, he grew heavy on her shoulder and fell to the ground, lights out. She checked his pulse and breathing. Both steady.

Thinking of what to do next, she re-entered the house to get her backpack from upstairs. In the mudroom, she lifted Toodles from the floor and carefully tucked him inside the pack. She didn't want to leave him behind.

Far off, sirens bayed. She went out to Paul, still senseless on the grass. Once the sirens sounded like they'd reached the cul-de-sac, she started across the yard, her backpack pulling on her shoulders.

All the way to Lucinda's, she kept glancing behind her, expecting a cop car or the dealer's goon. She thought of Paul running into the house to rescue her and felt no gratitude, only anger. She pictured Ülle bashing him with the golf club, then ripping open the trash bag. Even if she'd opened it in time, she would blame Regan for abandoning them. Regan wanted to tell her that it wasn't her fault. It was her father's. Her mother's. Regan should call both of them and say she'd had enough. Their family was over. She was leaving and never coming back.

Except Lucinda could have called the cops, too. By now, Ülle and Jari might be sealed up dead with the baby. Regan increased her pace, letting the pain in her foot distract her from the thought.

Lucinda's house was on a boulevard lined with cottonwoods gone to seed, their white fluff choking the street in clumps. A pair of little girls were rolling balls of the stuff to build a late spring snowman on their lawn. Lucinda's house stood four doors down from them, the biggest on the block, with a garage in a separate coach house. The floodlight at the side of the coach house had been left on, even though the sun still hung in the sky. Maybe it was a signal.

Regan was about to investigate when the house's front door opened and Lucinda leaned out, beckoning her. Regan broke into a jog and hurried inside.

'You asshole,' said Lucinda as she closed the door. 'You ordered a flatpack? What were you thinking?' She pulled her into a hug.

'I'm sorry,' Regan whispered. Then she drew back. 'Are they here?' She was picturing the trash bag, the steak knife, the green-streaked walls.

Lucinda nodded. 'They're in the coach house.'

'Are they all right?'

'Well, I mean, they're scared. Some guy stabbed Jari. The cuts are pretty shallow, though.'

It was strange to hear Jari's name coming from her lips.

'What about the baby?' Regan asked.

'The baby's fine – no thanks to the guy, apparently.'

'It wasn't just a guy,' said Regan. 'It was Paul, trying to save me.'

Lucinda's eyes went full manga. 'Is he okay?' she said. 'Ülle said she nailed him with a golf club.'

'He'd passed out when I got there, but he woke up, kind of. I called 911, then took off. God, I'm awful, aren't I?'

Lucinda looked like she was weighing the possibility. 'Come on,' she said, turning to go further into the house. 'They're worried about you.'

'I thought they were in the coach house,' said Regan.

'They are, but it's better not to use the front door. Ülle said you have a stalker now?'

As they passed through the house, Regan wondered what Lucinda was thinking. In her place, Regan would have taken one look at Ülle and Jari and barricaded herself in the house. She remembered the time in biology class when the frogs had caught on fire. Lucinda had been the one to grab the extinguisher and calmly douse the flames. Afterwards, Regan had asked her how she'd kept it together, and Lucinda had said the trick was to empty yourself, imagine you weren't a person but a function, a role, a set of actions to be carried out. Regan had said it sounded dandy, but when Lucinda was busy being just a function, where did the rest of her go?

Lucinda had said she didn't know.

In the living room, Lucinda opened the sliding door to the patio and gestured for Regan to step outside. Once they'd reached the coach house and were about to mount the staircase to the suite above the garage, Regan asked her to wait.

'I wanted to tell you, I'm sorry for sending them here,' Regan said. 'It wasn't Plan A, but I had to look after my dad, and I figured if there was anybody they'd be safe with – '

'Don't sweat it.' Lucinda flashed a smile before turning serious. 'Ülle said you're immune to them. That true?'

'Seems like it. Why? You didn't spend time inside with them, did you?'

'Not at first, but then I ran a little experiment. We stayed in the kitchen for twenty minutes.'

The recklessness of it made Regan grit her teeth. 'You didn't have a reaction? No buzz? No coughing? Did you check your skin?'

Lucinda held out her arms for Regan's inspection. There was nothing visible.

'Twenty minutes isn't long enough to be sure,' Regan said. 'You shouldn't take risks.'

Lucinda nodded, looking unconcerned. 'If I start to feel funny, I'll let you know.'

They started up the stairs to the suite. Once upon a time, Lucinda's parents had used it for houseguests, but Lucinda had claimed it for herself a few days before coming out. It remained mostly as her father had first decorated it, a single room with caribou antlers and criss-crossed fishing rods on the walls. The pelt of some poor creature lay draped over the backrest of a wicker loveseat, and there was a coffee table made of birch branches still wrapped in bark. Lucinda's father was an oil company executive from Kenya. She said the decor had been his idea of a joke.

When she and Regan entered, they found Ülle and Jari sitting on the loveseat, Ülle with the baby against her chest. She and Jari were wearing baseball caps that Regan recognized as her father's, and Jari sported a button-down that Regan had never seen before. The other shirt must have been ruined when Paul stabbed him. Wherever the wounds were, they didn't show.

Ülle gave Regan a nod of greeting, but Jari was busy staring at the framed image on the wall behind him. It was the portrait of Regan that Lucinda had painted when they were together, a gaudy mix of charcoal and tempera for which Regan had posed nude after Lucinda convinced her it would be the hottest thing ever. In fact, it had been eight hours of itchiness and bottled farts. Lucinda had declared it her masterpiece, but the image of the bony girl with bad skin and a pissed-off pout had left Regan suspecting that Lucinda hated her, and she'd made her promise never to exhibit it. The next evening, Regan had arrived at the coach house to find the portrait hanging in the place it now occupied, a plain black dress painted over her body's likeness. Two days after that, Lucinda had broken up with her.

When Regan called out a hello, Jari emerged from his reverie and bounded toward her.

'Papa!' he cried. 'Papa, Papa!' There was barely time to set her backpack on the floor before he knocked into her.

Ülle approached at a slower pace, still holding the baby. He'd been swaddled in a beach towel, so that Regan could see only his tousled red hair. He didn't move or make a sound, and Regan suddenly felt ill.

'Do not worry,' said Ülle. 'He is sleeping. Before you came, we fed him milk.'

'He's all right?' Regan said. 'How long did he spend in the trash bag?'

'Only a few seconds. He was still crying when I took him out. A good sign, no?'

Regan agreed that it was.

Ülle turned so that Regan could see the baby's face, his eyelids shut tight, his lips peacefully askew, his silvery cheek mushed into Ülle's shoulder. Lucinda and Jari looked upon him, too, and even Jari seemed to appreciate the sanctity of the hush that came over all of them.

'Baby!' he said, but in a whisper, as if sharing his most precious secret.

Then Ülle gazed down at Regan's backpack.

'You have brought the cat?' she said.

Regan wondered how she knew. Maybe she'd noticed the care with which Regan had set the pack on the floor. She expected

Ülle to disapprove, but judging by her expression, she only felt sorry for her.

'Kitty cat?' said Jari. When he bent down toward the pack, Regan grabbed his arm and pulled him back up. He gave a little whine but returned his attention to the baby.

A moment later, Lucinda laid her hand on Regan's shoulder. 'Ülle told me what happened to Toodles,' she said. 'I'm sorry.'

The sadness in her voice was a surprise. During their time together, she hadn't shown much interest in Toodles. Although she'd pleaded allergies, Regan had always wondered if they were just an excuse for Lucinda not to spend time at Regan's house, to keep the relationship on her own turf and terms.

'What will you do with him?' Ülle asked.

'I don't know,' said Regan. 'Bury him, I guess.'

'If you want, you can do it here,' Lucinda said. 'Or I can do it for you.'

The idea made sense. Who knew when they'd get another chance? But as Regan opened her mouth to agree, she hesitated. Leaving Toodles to rest eternally in Lucinda's backyard didn't feel right, not when Lucinda had been ghosting her. Regan needed a promise that she could visit him whenever she liked or something, but she couldn't ask for that. It would sound like a ploy to wangle her way back into Lucinda's life.

'Yes, please bury him,' said Ülle to Lucinda. With her free hand, she picked up the backpack. 'Will you go with Jari and do it now?'

'Wait, hold on,' said Regan. 'I need to think about this.' She reached out to reclaim the backpack, but before she could, Ülle gave it to Lucinda.

'I must speak with you,' Ülle said, turning to Regan. 'Let them go and do this.'

'But somebody might see Jari,' Regan protested.

'It'll be okay,' said Lucinda. 'There are hedges, remember?'

Regan remembered the hedges. She remembered staring up at them with Lucinda one night in the summer, as they lay on their backs in the darkness.

Lucinda put on the backpack and took Jari by the hand. In response, he turned to Ülle with a scandalized look, but Ülle only gave him a nod of encouragement.

'Go with her,' she said. 'Help her dig the hole.' To Lucinda, she added, 'It is easy to upset him. Maybe do not talk about what you bury.'

Ülle waited until Lucinda and Jari had descended the stairs. Then she lifted the baby from her chest and pressed him into Regan's. Regan felt his chubby chin settle on her collarbone. Even through the towel's swaddle, she could feel the nudge of his niblet toes against her stomach.

'He is not my baby,' Ülle announced.

Regan needed a second to realize what she'd said. 'Are you sure? What happened? Did you remember something?'

'I just know it. I knew it the moment the man took him from me in your house.'

At the thought, Regan felt a surge of guilt. 'The man was Paul. My other ex.'

'He did not say his name,' Ülle replied. 'But he kept asking where you were.'

'Will you tell me what happened?' said Regan.

A look of distress came over Ülle.

'If you don't want to talk about it – ' Regan began.

'No, it is fine.' Ülle spoke the words as if willing them to be truthful. Then she went to the loveseat, and Regan sat down beside her.

'While we waited for you, there was a knocking,' said Ülle. 'I do not know who it is, so I take Jari and the baby to hide. We are running to the basement when I see that Jari has dropped his golfing stick. Before I can pick it up, your Paul comes inside. He points a knife, tells us to get in the bathroom. I am thinking we will wait for a chance to escape, but Jari jumps at your Paul like a little dog, and your Paul cuts him.'

'God, I'm sorry,' said Regan. 'I never should have left – '

Ülle waved away her apology. 'Your Paul takes the baby. He puts Jari and me in the bathroom and keeps the door shut with a chair, but we are stronger than he thinks. We push the chair out of the way. I hit your Paul with the golfing stick and take the baby from the bag. Then we run away.'

Regan felt like throwing up. 'Paul didn't know what he was doing,' she said. 'He just wanted to stop the fumes.'

The baby stirred against her and made a hiccuppy sound. Ülle leaned forward, as if to reclaim him at the first sign of trouble, but he only fell back into sleep. Regan began running through everything that had happened to her while she was gone, trying to determine what Ülle needed to know, and landed upon her encounter with the dealer's goon.

'You sure you don't remember more?' she asked. 'Nothing about you and Jari?'

Ülle shook her head. 'Why do you ask it like that?'

'Because I had a run-in with the guy driving the van. I asked him if your names were Ülle and Jari, and he didn't answer, but I swear, his eyes popped out of his head.'

Ülle turned to gaze at Regan's portrait with a pained look.

'If you want, I'll help you try to find out who you are,' said Regan.

Ülle gave a little smile and shrugged. 'Whatever my life was, I wished to leave it, no? Is it not how flatpacking worked? The people agreed to be sent off?' She rose from the loveseat. 'Right now, we must talk about what comes next. Did your Lucinda tell you what she discovers?'

Regan shook her head.

'There is a place for flatpacked people,' Ülle said. 'A safe place, a secret place, in the west.'

Regan frowned. In all her reading about flatpacks, she'd never seen a hint of such a thing. 'How did she find out?' she asked, and Ülle said she didn't know.

They agreed to go talk with Lucinda, and Ülle took the baby from Regan to let her get up more easily. Even before they reached the stairs, Regan was already sorting through possible next steps. Then her phone buzzed. It was a text from Paul. '*Where ru?*'

He was okay then. At least, okay enough to text her. Except it might be the cops using his phone.

Her phone began to ring. Paul again. She dismissed the call and turned off the phone. The cops could be trying to track her, or the dealer's goon could be doing the same.

'We have to leave,' she told Ülle.

Outside, they found Lucinda with a shovel and Jari with a spade, the two of them filling a shallow hole in a corner of the yard. Ülle passed the baby to Regan, then reached for the shovel in Lucinda's hands.

'I will finish it,' Ülle said. 'Tell Regan about the place in the west.'

Lucinda gave her the shovel, and Ülle joined Jari in the task of piling dirt.

'There's some kind of flatpack sanctuary?' Regan said.

'They're cagey about the location,' Lucinda replied. 'It's someplace in the New Nations, in the mountains. I found out about it online.'

'I never heard of it,' said Regan.

Lucinda's eyebrows went up a little. 'That's because you think the whole internet can be googled.'

'But why would there be a sanctuary if flatpacks die after a week?'

'That's just the new ones, remember? Seems like some of the older ones managed to avoid the roundup.'

It sounded too good to be true.

'What if it's a hoax?' Regan said.

'I don't know, babes. What other choice is there?'

Regan paused before she spoke. 'I was thinking maybe your cabin.'

Lucinda's expression moved from surprise to something like pity. 'That won't work,' she said. 'Some friends of my parents are up there.'

She sounded relieved to have the excuse. A moment later, her phone rang. She pulled it out and checked the number.

'It's Paul,' she said. 'You want me to answer?'

Regan didn't know. Ignoring his text had made sense, but it might be a mistake for Lucinda to ignore him, too.

The phone kept ringing. Regan felt the baby tense against her ribs. She turned away, trying to shield him from the noise. Ülle had stopped digging and took a few steps in Lucinda's direction.

'Answer,' she said. 'Or Paul will be suspecting.'

Lucinda answered, then listened.

'No, I haven't heard from her,' she said after a time. Again, she listened. 'Oh my God. How can I help?'

Just then, Jari cried out in a keening voice. 'Kitty caaaat!'

He'd piled the last of the dirt back into the grave.

'Jari, shush,' whispered Ülle.

'Sorry, just some weirdo on the street,' said Lucinda into the phone. She listened some more. 'Sure, if she does, I'll let you know.' She tapped her phone and tucked it away.

'You think he knew it was Jari?' Regan asked.

'Better not stick around and risk it,' said Lucinda.

Ülle went to take Jari by the hand and looked ready to leave right then.

'Where will you go?' Lucinda asked.

'Don't know,' said Regan. 'The bus station? The dealer stole my dad's car.'

'I heard. Why don't you take my parents' Volvo?'

It was what Regan had hoped for, but it didn't feel right. More like a blow-off than a kindness. The easiest way to be rid of her.

'No, you'd get in trouble,' she said.

'What am I, twelve? Take it.'

Lucinda was always like this, giving you things but spoiling the gifts. On Regan's birthday, she'd bought her a fancy dinner, even though Regan hated restaurants. Another time, Lucinda had carped about the hours she'd spent baking her an apple soufflé, yet she still expected her to eat some, as if unable to see how all her complaining had ruined it. After a while, her fuck-ups felt intentional, a way of telling Regan that she wanted the wrong things. Well, they didn't need her cabin or her car.

'Come on,' Regan said to Ülle. 'Let's get going.'

Ülle looked confused. 'Without the car? How will we go to the station?'

'Fine, we'll take the Volvo.' Regan turned back to Lucinda. 'That okay?'

Lucinda was staring at her with a worried expression. 'Babes, have you eaten anything today?' she said.

The question filled Regan with rage. Before she could manage an answer, Lucinda spoke to Ülle.

'Will you go to the kitchen and pack some food?' she said. 'We'll be there in a second.'

Ülle gave a murmur of assent. Letting go of Jari, she went to Regan and took the baby from her. Regan didn't know how Ülle would pack food while holding the kid, and she wondered if Ülle didn't trust her to look after him. Or maybe Ülle just didn't want to let him out of her sight.

Once she'd carried him through the sliding door with Jari in tow, Lucinda turned back to Regan with a pained expression.

'Regan, do you really want to run off with these people? Before Ülle and Jari were flatpacked, they could have been anybody. Scammers, murderers – '

'You think Ülle's a murderer?'

'You know what I mean.'

Regan bit her lip, because what she wanted to say was something Lucinda would never agree to. Yet knowing as much somehow made it easier to suggest. 'You could come with us,' she said.

'Oh, sweetheart. I don't think that's a good idea.'

It was the answer Regan had expected, but it still hurt. She decided to keep going, anyhow. 'You said yourself, they don't seem to be affecting you. We can drive with the windows rolled down. If you start reacting, we can drop you off somewhere.'

Why was it so necessary to make a fool of herself? Lucinda glanced toward the house as if eager to be inside.

'Never mind,' Regan said. 'Forget I mentioned it.'

They listened to the snarl of a lawn mower a few houses over. Their shadows stretched across the grass, and Lucinda whacked at a mosquito on her leg.

'Will you tell me something?' Regan said. 'Why is that painting of me still up?'

'I'm sorry,' Lucinda replied. 'I wasn't expecting you to see it.'

As soon as she said it, Regan realized what she'd just admitted: she hadn't planned to have her over ever again. 'That doesn't answer the question,' said Regan. 'Why not take it down?'

Lucinda let out a sigh. 'It's just that it's the best thing I've done.'

Regan didn't believe her. Some part of Lucinda must still want her around. Not the real her, though: a tidier version. One that would never complain or make demands. The portrait's stomach wouldn't growl during movies. A painting wouldn't weep for no reason or drive off with the family car.

'Let's go inside,' Regan said. 'We'd better see what they're up to.'

Lucinda glanced back at the grave, the shovel and spade lying abandoned beside it. 'You want some time on your own out here? You know, to say goodbye to him?'

Regan shook her head. She didn't think she could handle it right now. 'You'll let me come back, won't you?' she said, and Lucinda nodded. 'Then I'll wait until then.'

She tried to focus on next steps. They needed enough things for the baby to get them through the first few hours of driving.

They needed whatever further information Lucinda could offer about the sanctuary. They needed a cash machine to avoid leaving a credit-card trail. After that, they could hit the road.

When she followed Lucinda into the house, though, even before they entered the kitchen, something wasn't right. It was the lack of noise, then the rumble of a vehicle's engine, louder than it should have been, as if a window at the front had been left open. She looked at Lucinda and saw her frowning, too.

They went into the kitchen and found it deserted. On the counter sat a shopping bag half-filled with food. A jar of preserves lay on the floor, cracked in two and leaking dark liquid. Regan caught a whiff of ozone, like a fuse box had blown.

Lucinda called out and got no response.

'Check upstairs,' said Regan, filling with dread. 'I'll look down here.'

In the bathroom and the dining room, she found no trace of them. Upon reaching the hallway, she saw that the front door was open. A man stood straddling the jamb.

The dealer's goon.

The two of them locked eyes. When he started toward her, Regan turned and ran.

His footsteps followed her, growing louder. She heard him puffing and could swear she felt his breath. Making it to the living room seemed a miracle. She flung open the sliding door and booked it across the patio, dodged a deck chair, leapt over another. As she landed, she expected a calamity in her foot, but adrenaline muzzled the pain. She hit the lawn and tore across it. The speed she could still manage! She felt her airways widening, her whole sensorium opening up, the smell of lilac and coltsfoot in bloom, her legs registering nothing but the pleasure of movement.

As she made the side of the house, she was hit by a weird certainty of what was to come. The beige van sat parked in front, and Ülle and Jari were locked inside it with the baby. The goon had left the key in the ignition. Regan was going to beat him there, beat him by inches, jump in the driver's seat, and drive the motherfucker to freedom.

The force of her conviction was so strong that she didn't quite believe it when he stepped around the corner to block her path, pointing what looked like a toy gun, a phaser, something pure science fiction.

She didn't see him pull the trigger. There was just a white-out blast of pain. She toppled to the ground, body planking, every muscle knotted. A rat-a-tat crackle came from a pair of wires that double-helixed from the goon's gun to her body. When it stopped, she had a vague awareness of him lifting her off the ground and slinging her over his shoulder.

'I told you to be good,' he said. 'I should have known. Nobody ever listens to me.'

EIGHT

LETTER TO LITTLE ONE

Little one, let me tell you how Ülle tried to be a hero. It didn't start well, for what kind of hero gets lost when trying to save the day? As she directed the cab driver on the way to the warehouse, she couldn't remember the route. The first time she'd travelled there, she'd been distracted by Itzy's reckless driving and her carsickness. During the trip home, she'd been preoccupied by the warehouse happenings. Now, after half a dozen wrong turns, the driver grew impatient. Each time Ülle issued a new direction, he gave an insubordinate grunt.

Why does it matter to you whether I get it right? she asked. If I'm wrong, you'll just be paid more.

At last, the warehouse appeared. Itzy's van was the only vehicle in the parking lot. As the cab came to a stop, she counted out a handful of bills. Even in her state of distraction, she worried about the tip. In the end, she added an extra twenty dollars to establish herself as the bigger person.

The driver had peeled out of the lot by the time she tried the warehouse door and found it locked. When she hammered on it, no one answered. Circling the building, she searched for another entrance. Finally, she hauled a cinder block from a pile of rubble and heaved it through the closest window. After clearing away the shards of glass still clinging to the frame, she eased herself through the aperture. Inside, the main space was deserted, but the lights in the white-walled room were on, and she could hear a loud hum coming from it.

When she entered the room, the hum's intensity grew so strong that she found it hard to see. Is that even possible, little one? Can a noise be so loud that it not only deafens but also blinds? That's how it seemed to Ülle. Through narrowed eyes, she saw the flatpacked bodies stacked against the wall. She saw the vat of green liquid, which appeared to be the source of the humming as it churned and bubbled. She thought she caught a glimpse of a shape briefly bobbing to the surface.

Itzy lay stretched out on his back across a metal table. The left sleeve of his shirt had been rolled up, and his right hand held a long syringe. She watched him until she caught the rise and fall of his chest. Then she turned and saw Jari hunched over in a chair. His eyes were open and fixed on her, his body motionless. She hurried to his side.

Are you all right? she shouted over the hum. Can you move?

He only sat there in his slump. She checked his pulse and found it even. His eyes looked back at hers with the semblance of a conscious mind directing them.

Can you hear me? she said. Blink if you understand.

She drew back and saw him blink.

Did he give you a pill? she asked. An injection?

He blinked again.

He must have injected himself, too, she said. I'm going to get you out of here.

In reply, his eyelids fluttered. She could guess what it meant. He didn't want to leave. Whatever was happening, it was how he desired it. Well, she didn't care.

He was heavier than Ülle by some margin. The only way she might manage to remove him from the building was if she dragged him. Taking him by the armpits, she worked him sideways until he dropped to the floor. The rough concrete surface tugged his shirt up as she pulled him toward the doorway. A trail of blood began to appear behind him. She told herself that his skin would heal; the important thing was to get him far away.

By the time they reached the parking lot, sweat had soaked her through. The winter air bit at her flesh. Itzy's van sat invitingly, but she didn't have the keys and couldn't bear the thought of re-entering the building to search for them. Instead, she left Jari by the warehouse door and crossed the lot to hail a cab. It took a long time before one appeared. She told the driver that Jari had been drinking, and she asked for the man's help in lifting him into the back of the car.

She was about to climb in, too, when she remembered the baby. She stuck her head into the car, feeling the warmth of its interior.

Is the baby in the warehouse? she whispered to Jari.

He blinked once.

Is he in danger? she asked.

He blinked again, and her heart sank.

I'll go back for him, she said.

She gave the driver their address and paid him twice what the ride should cost. It felt wrong to send Jari off by himself, but she didn't want to risk him staying at the warehouse and coming out of his paralysis while still intent on being flatpacked. The cab returned to the street and drove away. A cloud cocooned the sun, making her shiver. She turned and went back inside the building.

Once in the white-walled room again, she scanned it for the baby. It took her a moment to realize that Itzy's body was gone from the table. In the same instant, something stung her in the neck. Her legs went from under her. She saw a syringe fall to the ground. A man's hands kept her upright. She knew as he carried her across the room that it was Itzy.

He sat her in a chair and peered at her with concern.

Quick, while you can still talk, he said. Where is Jari?

She tried to curse him, but her jaw had stopped working, and her tongue seemed to have swollen to fill her mouth.

He swore and ran from the room. She was unable even to turn her head and watch him leave. A minute later, he returned in a panic.

What have you done? he screamed. He and I were to go together! It's too late now, I'm lost. I gave myself the unction.

He paced about the room, looking behind tables and machinery, as if Jari might be hidden there. Then he noticed the blood on the floor.

You dragged him, did you? he said. Your precious Jari didn't want any pain, he wanted to be paralyzed before the unction. That's your man for you, a coward, a poltroon! Do you know how much the unction hurts? It takes your brain. Oh God, I feel mine going! Where is he? You horrid thing, you've ruined it! He'll die of the worm now. Is that what you wanted?

Ülle fought to speak, to demand that Itzy tell her of the baby.

Doesn't matter, Itzy murmured, looking at his watch. The foreman will be here soon to finish the job. Oh, but I refuse to go alone with that vile baby! You bitch, you've made me do such shameful things, you and Jari. He didn't have the nerve to go by himself. We made a pact!

Itzy began to weep great tears.

I don't want to go now, he cried. I don't want to!

Ülle could still move her eyes. They settled on the vat in the centre of the room. The hum from it had died, and the air above it waggled with heat lines. She caught another glimpse of something at the surface.

Itzy must have noticed the direction of her gaze.

Don't judge me! he said. I did it for Jari. We hadn't used the machinery yet, we had to test it. And look at the little scoundrel, now he'll live forever like his dear papa, he'll get to be the baby for eternity.

He glanced at his watch.

Oh, sweet Jesus! he cried. I'm so hungry! It's the unction. It gives you this awful emptiness. You should have heard the cries of the people at the factory. You couldn't feed them, it wasn't permitted, you just had to suffer through their noise.

He looked at her and scowled.

Stop staring like that, he said. You've taken Jari from me! Oh, but perhaps he'll come back. Please, God …

He ran out of the room again. Ülle returned her attention to the vat and saw a tiny shoulder break the surface, then submerge. When she tried to move, she found that she could flex the toes on her right foot. She wiggled them, hoping the action might revive the rest of her.

Itzy returned with a look of frenzied purpose. He crossed the room to a place outside her field of vision. There was the sound of a refrigerator door opening and closing, then the clink of things being set on a table.

Lucky girl, he said. Won't feel a thing.

Only a minute passed before she heard him approach her from behind. She tried to shout at him not to touch her, but her throat was a column of stone.

There, he said after a time. I've given you the unction. Now there's no turning back.

It began a second later, a hunger in her belly, growing more quickly than any craving she'd ever felt.

Don't worry, he said. When my cousin sees you, he'll want to be flatpacked, too. Even if he doesn't, you and I will have each other. Maybe they'll wake us in a hundred years. Wouldn't that be a trick? We'll be quite the couple. You're such a pretty girl. I always said he was lucky to get you.

She listened to him press buttons on his phone.

Jari, it's your dear cousin, he said after a pause. You must come back to the warehouse. Three lives depend on it! If Ülle could speak now, she'd tell you she made a mistake in removing you. Come back, make sure the foreman has done his job, and join us. Things are working out better than you planned, for now you'll have your woman with you, too.

He hung up and promptly abandoned his jocularity in favour of more swearing and shouting at the walls. Then she felt herself being lifted into the air.

Time for the vat, he said. Christ, I'm famished! I've never felt such hunger.

By that point, she could move her right foot from the ankle down, but it did no good. Itzy brought her to the vat and leaned her against the side.

I'll tell you the plain truth, he said. I knew Jari would be unhappy about the pipsqueak, so I carried out my experiment before he arrived. Jari raised such a stink when he found out, it made the paralysis quite necessary. When you receive the unction, you must be relaxed.

He scooped her off the ground and slid her over the edge of the vat. The sensation was returning to her skin, so that she could feel the heat of the green liquid on her ankles, her knees, her midriff as he lowered her in.

It should be Jari, not you, said Itzy. This isn't what I wanted. If you remember one thing, remember that.

She felt him release her. She floated on her back in the green brine, and the baby's body nudged against her.

One more call, Itzy exclaimed, bringing out his phone. He must have been sent through to voice mail again, because he left a long, uninterrupted rebuke of someone named Carel for being late, then an explanation about a change of plans and the fact that it was a woman's body, not Jari's, that would be found alongside his and the baby's.

The foreman, he explained after hanging up. He'll take care of the final stages. So even if our Jari doesn't return, my dear, you and I have a chance.

He groaned and swung a leg over the edge of the vat.

This hunger is killing me! he cried.

Her body rose with the displacement of liquid as he slid in beside her. When he put his arms around her torso, she felt the baby lodged between them. Together, the three of them began to sink. The hot green wooze ran into her mouth.

Drink it up, she heard him say. The change will go more quickly.

He didn't speak again.

Little one, I can't say for certain what happened after that. I can't tell you whether, on Jari's return to the factory, he wept and cursed his cousin's name. I can't tell you if it was Jari or the foreman or the two together who carried out the last procedures. But whatever happened, that day was the end of Ülle – or, at least, the end of her as she was then.

At the start of telling you all this, I worried that I wouldn't get it down in time. I was afraid that what had once been taken from me would somehow be snatched away again. I can't call it memory. It feels like someone else's life. Still, I wanted to save what was left of her before she disappeared.

Except things haven't gone like that. Instead of vanishing, she's closer. Ever since I began writing, my nights have been filled by dreams of her: Ülle hounded by the thud of weights; Ülle in the taxi, searching for the warehouse. The more I've written, the more doggedly she has followed me into sleep. At first, I thought she pursued me in anger. I feared I'd got things wrong. She has never turned against me, though. Perhaps she stalks me only with caring, hoping I won't waste this do-over life.

Little one, I care for you so much! I, who thought I could never devote myself to a little one again. What will you make of this Ülle I've given you? Part of me hopes that you'll cast a cold eye on her so you can avoid a fate such as hers. But another part hopes that you'll love her, close as she and I are. Because I do want to be loved by you, little one, with as much faith and gusto as I love you. Who can predict how long we'll accompany each other in this life? All I know is that whenever our time comes, it will be better if we go with love.

NINE

CONSPIRATOR

Alone in the pitch-black back of the van, Regan tried to keep track of the turns the vehicle was making, but her body hurt too much. Even when her arms and legs began to work again, they ached. She reached for her phone and couldn't find it. She crawled to the cargo doors and turned the handles. Locked. She imagined beating on the van's walls. No, the goon would pull over and tase her again, or worse. Besides, just trying to open the doors had exhausted her. Sprawling across the floor to rest, she listened for noises from outside that might reveal their location, but she heard only generic traffic sounds. She wondered what had happened to Ülle, Jari, and the baby. They could be in the van, too, sitting beside the goon with a gun pointed at them, waiting for their moment to escape.

Maybe half an hour passed before the van came to a stop, the engine shut off, and there was the sound of the driver's door opening and closing. By that point, the pain had faded, and she moved to the back of the van, ready to dry-gulch him if she got the chance. No sooner had the cargo doors swung open than he dropped her with the taser. A bag went over her head, and he hoisted her into the air.

He set her down and removed the bag in what appeared to be a storage closet. Regan found herself squinting at cinder-block walls and a bare light bulb. The goon looked her over, seeming mildly concerned, like a mourner at a funeral gazing at a distant cousin's corpse. Then he left, locking the door behind him.

Why had he brought her here? After what had happened with Paul, the police would be searching for her. The goon must know that. Maybe he meant to abandon her in the room forever. She struggled to her feet, muscles screaming, and banged her fists against the door. Maybe Ülle and Jari were locked up nearby with the baby. She yelled Ülle's name and listened in vain for a response.

The room was cold and airless, empty even of shelves. The floor stank of cleaning solvents. She was hungry and dog-tired. Every part of her body hated her. It hurt to stand, but she had nowhere to sit or lie except the concrete floor, nothing to do except pace in a tight square and go through her stretching routine, trying to figure out what she'd say to the dealer if she got the chance. She couldn't decide how to explain leaving the house and whether it would be worth the risk to tell bald-faced lies.

At least an hour had gone by when the door opened and a figure in an orange hazmat suit entered the room. It was the goon, his teeth glinting through the face shield. In his hands was a rolled-up flatpack wrapped in plastic.

Regan assumed the flatpack was Ülle. The idea made no sense; in all Regan's reading, nobody had even mentioned reflattening. But when the goon set down the package and sliced it open with a box cutter, she began to imagine blowing into her again. A whole chain of events linked together in her mind. When the opportunity arose, she and Ülle would flee the building and hail a cab. Lucinda would dip into her trust fund to buy the two of them a boat, and they'd sail down the Gichigami River to the sea, then south along the Atlantic coast to some island owned by a Hollywood star who never stayed there. Maybe Lucinda would even join them.

That, or Regan and Ülle would remain captives here forever. It might not be so bad. The same bowl of gruel three times a day. Endless sit-ups, the two of them urging each other on until their abs were waffle irons. A life trimmed down to manageable dimensions, the kind that Regan imagined her father enjoying at the treatment centre. After she'd first learned of that place, she'd told her mother in a joking way that she wanted to check in, too.

'Oh, you couldn't,' her mother had replied. 'Not until he can get by on his own.'

After pulling the rolled-up body from the package, the goon spread it out across the floor. The person who emerged looked nothing like Ülle. It was a man unknown to her, with long dark hair and a scruff of beard on a pruney face. He lay naked on his back, his dick tucked up beneath him.

'Don't inflate him or I'll break your fingers,' said the goon.

'Who is he?' Regan asked.

The goon didn't answer.

'I'm hungry,' she said. 'I need the bathroom.'

The goon only retrieved the plastic wrapping from the floor and left. The flatpacked man lay there with his eyes and mouth open and unmoving. The patches of flattened hair on him were already starting to spring up.

Now that she'd been told not to inflate him, she could think of nothing else. Why would the goon just leave him there? Maybe they were testing her immunity to flatpacks, or maybe it was a weird kind of torture, sticking her with someone who wouldn't provide company. Well, if that was their plan, they were on the wrong track. She didn't need some dude to chat with.

Maybe the guy would know something, though. Even if he didn't, he might help her take down the goon. But if she inflated him, then he might have only a few days to live. Except he might have only a few days now anyhow; she couldn't remember whether it was the unwrapping or the inflating that started them dying. Then again, her imperviousness to Ülle and Jari could be due to some change in the manufacturing process in response to the worm's mutation. Maybe it also meant that flatpacks no longer died right away. Ülle and Jari might live for years and years.

Before she could decide what to do, there was the sound of a key in the lock again. The goon entered in his hazmat suit and handed her a wooden salad bowl along with a family-sized bag of potato chips.

'Can I open the chips?' she said. 'Or are they like the flatpacked guy, and I have to let them sit here, too?'

The goon gave a weary laugh, as though he'd had a long day. 'There's your bathroom,' he said, pointing to the salad bowl.

'You're kidding me,' she said.

'It's that or the floor.' He turned to leave.

'Are Ülle and Jari and the baby okay?' she said. When he didn't reply, she added, 'Will you at least tell me how you found us?'

He stayed motionless with his back to her, until she figured that he must be inwardly raging, but when he spoke, he only sounded smug.

'Your computer,' he said. 'Somebody had used it to search for your friend's address.'

Before she could ask him how he'd accessed her computer, he left the room.

After a while, she peed into the salad bowl, keeping her eyes on the flatpacked guy in case he somehow gained consciousness. Then she opened the chips. Sour cream and onion. She hated sour cream and onion. Inside a minute, half the bag was down her throat. When only a few broken bits remained, she realized that it might be some time before she got more to eat and she should save the rest. She still felt hungry, though. That was always the problem. She could never tell what amount of food was right. If she let herself eat until she felt full, she got fat. If she stopped at what seemed reasonable, her hunger never went away.

She dry-drank the rest of the chips and cleaned out the bag with a wet finger. Tiredness rolled over her. Lying down on the floor, she closed her eyes. Eventually, the walls gave way and she was in her bedroom, her mother hollering from outside the door that Regan had to go to the birthday party, she couldn't spend her life moping for no reason. When Regan went to let her mother in, nobody was there, and the house had a set of rooms she didn't remember. She became so involved in searching for her parents that it surprised her to wake up. A shadow passed across her face. The goon stood above her in his hazmat suit, looking twice as big as before. The room had gained a pea-green tinge, and the flatpacked man still lay a few feet away.

'Go back to sleep,' said the goon. Except it wasn't his voice coming from the hazmat suit; it was a woman's. She had a European accent, not quite the same as Ülle's. Regan turned her head just in time to see her slip out through the door.

The next time Regan woke, it was to her own coughing. Her throat burned. Her mouth was desert dry, and her eyes smarted in the haze. There were pink lesions on her arms, the skin pursed like she'd sprouted little sets of lips. The flattened man remained beside her, eyes and mouth agape. She wasn't immune then. But it wasn't supposed to hurt like this.

Gaining her feet, she made her way to the door and smashed at it, shouting to be let out, coughing whenever she tried to draw a proper breath.

Keeping upright took too much effort. She lay down again and found the haze even thicker at ground level. Covering her mouth with her hands, she curled into a ball. A pressure fattened in her ears, and a band around her forehead tightened. The lesions nipped and gnashed, yet her limbs seemed distant. The world was slipping away. She was in her room again, calling for her parents. No, it wasn't real. You could die in a dream if you let yourself. She had to break out before it dwindled her to nothingness.

She didn't know how long she'd been lying there when the door slammed into her back. She looked up to see her mother's jeans and raincoat. A patch of red hair. A silver jawline firmly set. It was Ülle, reaching for her.

'Come,' said Ülle. 'We must hurry.'

Regan leapt to her feet in her imagination. In reality, she couldn't move. 'I'm sorry,' she whispered. 'I'm sick.'

Ülle pulled her up and shuffled her into a narrow corridor. As they made their way along it, Regan hacked and wheezed. She tried to move her legs, but Ülle was practically carrying her.

'Where are Jari and the baby?' Regan asked.

'He isn't Jari,' Ülle replied. 'Jari was someone else.' Her voice was filled with sorrow. Regan didn't understand, but she was in too much pain to ask anything else.

'The one you know is Itzy,' said Ülle. 'That's his real name. He and the baby are with Mormor now.'

Regan waited for her to explain who Mormor was. Then she realized that she'd lost her focus on walking, so that Ülle was just dragging her. Ülle stopped to get a better purchase.

'I will explain later,' Ülle said. 'Now we must leave. Mormor wishes you to die.'

Regan tried to get her legs moving, but they refused to obey, and the lesions on her arms were shrieking. She let Ülle pull her down the corridor toward a closed door at its end.

They'd almost reached it when someone shouted at them from behind, ordering them to stop. Regan recognized the voice as the goon's.

Ülle stopped and gently lowered Regan until she sat against the wall. The goon was in her sightline now, standing outside the room he'd put her in. He'd removed his hazmat suit, and he was pointing a pistol in their direction.

'I told Mormor from the start that you should be locked up, too,' he said to Ülle. 'She never takes me seriously.'

'Driver, let us go,' said Ülle. 'She's just a girl.'

The familiarity with which Ülle addressed him was confusing. Regan wondered if her time with the flatpacked guy had somehow muddled her brain.

'You know this jerk?' she said.

'I know much now,' Ülle replied. 'I've spoken with Mormor. She told me everything that happened to me.'

'Enough talk,' said the goon. 'Get moving.'

'Driver, I remember you,' said Ülle. 'Perhaps if you hadn't been wearing a mask, I would have recognized you even in Regan's house. Please, let us go. You were always a decent man.'

He gave a laugh. 'You remember that? Your eggs really are scrambled.'

'It wasn't you who did this to me,' Ülle said. She gazed down at her silver palms, then held them out for his inspection. He stared at them with a pained look.

'No, it wasn't me,' he replied, his voice hard. 'I liked you well enough. It was that son of a bitch Itzy.'

Ülle nodded as if this fact, too, was something she knew. Then a flash of realization crossed her face. 'It was you who drew the moustache on Itzy, wasn't it?' she said.

Driver broke into a grin. 'Couldn't have been me,' he said with a wink. 'Mormor wouldn't like me doing that sort of thing. I just follow orders.' Then he turned sober. 'After she heard what Itzy had done, she got me to help Carel seal the two of you up.' He paused, seemingly troubled. 'The baby, too,' he added.

The hand holding the pistol dropped to his side. Eventually, he broke free of whatever memory had been gripping him.

'I can't believe you thought Itzy was Jari,' he said with disgust.

Ülle let out a sigh. 'I explained already. I was confused. I remembered only Jari's name.'

He shook his head. 'There's no use talking like this. Ülle's gone. You aren't her. You're someone else.'

'That isn't true,' she said. 'I'm her, a little more all the time. Much of what Mormor told me is coming back.'

Regan's head hurt from trying to follow. Was Mormor the dealer then? If the Jari that Regan knew was really called Itzy, where was the real Jari? She didn't even understand how Ülle knew these people. Regan wanted to demand that Ülle explain things from the beginning, but she knew that Ülle was trying to save her life right now, and she didn't want to interrupt.

Ülle reached for the door that she and Regan had been approaching. 'Please, let us go,' she said to Driver.

In return, he barked out words that sounded to Regan like gibberish. Ülle looked at him blankly, too.

'You see?' he said to her. 'You don't even remember your own language.'

He raised the gun again.

'Please, Driver.' Her fingers closed around the door handle.

The pistol fired. Regan covered her ears, too late, and a ringing filled her head. A little hole had appeared in the door not far from Ülle's hand.

'Come on,' he said. 'There's no point arguing. Mormor can see us.' He pointed to a camera mounted near the ceiling.

Ülle asked for his help in getting Regan back up the corridor, but he insisted on her doing it alone while he followed them. At the other end, the passageway opened out into an empty warehouse with tall windows and a cracked floor. They crossed the space to a room with white walls, fancy-looking equipment, and hot, soggy air. In the middle was an enormous vat filled with green liquid and covered with a glass lid. At the far end, an old woman nearly as large as the vat sat behind a metal desk. Her head had been shaved, and she had the most wrinkled face that Regan had ever seen, except the wrinkles weren't wrinkles. They were thick folds of skin, as if the woman had put on the face of someone with a head twice as big as hers and squashed it down to fit. She wore a grey dress that covered her arms to the elbows, revealing broad wattles on her forearms.

The woman was knitting what looked like a scarf. Standing next to her with a lopsided smile on his face, tossing and catching a red rubber ball, was Jari – Jari who wasn't Jari, after all, but Itzy, and apparently a total asshole.

'Papa!' he shouted. 'Mama!' Dropping the ball, he ran to them, and Ülle had to grab him by his shirt to keep him from jumping on Regan.

'Leave her,' Ülle told him. 'She is not well.'

They continued across the room with Regan still leaning on Ülle, Itzy close behind, and Driver trailing with his gun. As they drew closer to the old woman at the desk, Regan saw that behind her, a wooden crib stood against the wall. The baby lay on his stomach behind the bars, cooing as if everything was right with the world.

The old woman glowered at Itzy and told him to go play. After retrieving the rubber ball, he offered it to Driver, who rolled it along the ground for him. Itzy ran joyously to fetch it.

'An idiot,' said the woman in a low, hoarse voice. 'Itzy was so clever once.'

'I prefer this version,' said Ülle coolly.

'What would you know?' said the woman. 'You aren't so clever either. I go out of my way to be generous with you, and this is what you do.' She nodded toward a tablet on the desk, which showed camera views of various rooms and hallways. 'I told you that sparing the girl wasn't possible, but you had to have everything your way.'

'Mormor, you were killing her,' said Ülle.

'She ordered a flatpack,' the woman said. 'I was giving her what she wants.'

So this was Mormor. Regan had been right: she was the dealer. Regan tightened her grip on Ülle's shoulder. 'I changed my mind,' she announced. 'I don't want to die.'

Mormor stared at her as if she herself had gone through life never once changing her mind.

'I know what you are thinking, Mormor,' said Ülle. 'You think Regan doesn't matter because she isn't family. But who else is left?'

'You weren't so insolent before,' Mormor replied. 'I told you I would keep you, yet right away you test me.'

Mormor resumed her knitting, but her hands shook, and she stopped abruptly, as though keen for nobody to notice. Across the room, Driver kept throwing the ball for Itzy, and the stomp of Itzy's feet as he fetched it was almost as bad as the ringing in Regan's head.

'I don't owe you anything,' Mormor told Ülle. 'I did what I promised Jari. I kept you in this place when my only wish was to be rid of you.'

'You left us sealed in plastic,' said Ülle.

'What else could I do?' said Mormor. 'We thought there would be off-gassing like with all the others. I've already told you, Jari tried to fix the problem. He thought the machinery or the chemicals were to blame. It was only after he – ' Her throat seemed to close up. She rubbed it with both hands. 'Only once he was gone did we learn that the off-gassing had been caused by the worm mutating.' She stared down Ülle with heavy-lidded eyes. 'He wasted his last months like that. Trying to bring you back.'

Ülle returned her stare. 'You think it was a waste?' she asked.

Mormor hesitated. 'One must live with the living,' she said, like she was quoting someone.

'We were still alive,' said Ülle. 'When you learned about the mutation, why did you not unpack us? You knew we didn't have the worm, so the mutation couldn't have affected us. You knew we wouldn't pose any danger.'

'I didn't know it,' snapped Mormor. 'Itzy and the baby hadn't been tested. I never saw the results for you. Besides, why would I send you to the girl if I thought you wouldn't kill her?'

'Because you knew that even if we didn't die from the off-gassing, the police would kill us,' Ülle said. 'Then you could tell yourself that you were innocent, that it was only business. But the truth is, you just didn't want more Gretas on your hands, eating the dog's dinner and embarrassing you.'

Mormor looked startled by the words.

'Yes, I remember your confession about Greta, too,' said Ülle. 'Tell me, how long did you wait after Jari died before you broke your promise to him, selling me off, abandoning Itzy and the baby to a stranger?'

It didn't seem like a good idea for Ülle to be provoking Mormor as she was. Regan wanted to say something, but her ears still rang from the gunshot. Behind them, the sounds of the bouncing ball and Itzy's feet had stopped, as if he were waiting for Mormor to reply. From the crib, the baby still babbled away, indifferent to everything but his own monologue.

'What would you have done if we'd stayed at Regan's and kept living beyond seven days?' Ülle said to Mormor. 'Would you have had Driver return us to you?'

Mormor dropped her gaze.

'No, I didn't think so,' Ülle said.

'How could I know you would remember things?' Mormor muttered. 'I still don't understand. Some issue with the flatpacking, I suppose. It was their first time doing it in this place. But you and Itzy both went through it, and now only you are like this, while Itzy – '

Mormor picked up a knitting needle and poked it in his direction like she wanted to shish-kebab him. He bounded up to her happily, as if eager to facilitate the skewering. There was a look of weapons-grade hatred in Mormor's eyes, and for a second Regan thought that she might actually drive the needle through his skull. Instead, she used her other hand to push him away, and he hunted around the room until he found his ball again, then settled on the floor beside her.

'I am sorry that we did not turn out how you expected,' Ülle said to Mormor in an acid tone. 'I saw the man in the room where you kept Regan. Tell me, did you flatpack him recently? If so, let me offer congratulations. You have the process back to how it was. It will be so good for your business.'

'No, no,' said Mormor. 'The business is finished. Too few customers, too much trouble. That flatpack is from the factory in the old country. We needed to test the girl's resistance to the off-gassing.'

'And why was that?' said Ülle. Before Mormor could answer, she added, 'Don't say it, I know already. You wanted to see if Regan has some immunity that you lack. You weren't going to keep Itzy and me around if we might be a danger to you.'

Her rage seemed so white-hot that Regan wondered if it was a fake-out, a way of stalling until someone showed up to save them. Or maybe Ülle knew that Mormor wouldn't change her mind about Regan, and she was trying to delay the inevitable. It seemed funny, almost, that Ülle should be protecting her like this. She owed Regan no debt. If anything, it was the opposite. Regan had been the one to unseal and unflatten her. Because of her selfishness, Ülle might now have just a few days to live. Yet here she was, taking on Mormor while Regan leaned against her, as useful as a broken rubber band. Not that Ülle seemed to be getting anywhere. From the look on Mormor's face, nothing would dissuade her from doing with Regan what she planned.

The thought was too much to handle.

'If you let me go, I won't say anything,' Regan blurted.

All at once, Mormor and Ülle took on twin expressions of discomfort, like she'd made them ashamed on her behalf.

'Regan – ' said Ülle softly.

'We'll leave the city,' Regan went on. 'There's a flatpack sanctuary out west. We'll never bother you again.'

Regan felt Ülle tense, and it occurred to her that Ülle had wanted to keep the sanctuary a secret. She'd been holding out hope for them to reach the place without Mormor tracking them down. Regan had blown it – and for what? Her pleading had sounded pathetic, even in her own ears. She couldn't believe it when Mormor's brow wrinkled, like she was really considering whether to let them go.

'Is that where you were headed?' Mormor said to Ülle. 'Taking Itzy with you, after what he did?'

'You were right to say he isn't Itzy anymore,' Ülle replied. 'He doesn't remember what he did to me and the baby.' She watched him gnaw on the ball. 'Mormor, let us go to the sanctuary. It is what Jari would have wanted.'

'Jari?' Mormor said. 'Jari hated Itzy for what he did to you.' Her hands still trembled, and she seemed to have difficulty breathing. Regan could hear strings of phlegm in her voice. 'Jari cared about his Mormor, not Itzy. Shall I tell you why he didn't flatpack himself and join you? On his last day, he confessed it to me. He didn't want to leave me all alone.'

As she finished speaking, she pressed her hand to her temple. Her chest was heaving, and she'd gone pale. The baby had stopped its babbling, and Regan waited for it to break into a crying fit.

'Driver, I don't feel well,' Mormor said.

Then she slumped in her chair and toppled sideways. Itzy yelped and scrambled to get out of the way as she crashed to the floor.

Driver ran to where she lay, still clutching his pistol.

'Forgot my shot,' Mormor whispered.

He scuttled about her, seemingly fearful of setting down his gun to come to her aid. 'Help her,' he told Ülle. He was trying to sound tough, but his voice betrayed a quiver of panic.

Ülle seemed to weigh her options. Regan imagined her refusing, forcing Driver to help Mormor himself, then jumping him at the first chance. Except she had nobody to back her up. Regan could barely stand, and Itzy only looked on anxiously, like he cared about Mormor as much as Driver did.

'All right, I'll help,' said Ülle. She set Regan down in a chair opposite the desk. 'Where are Mormor's medicines?'

Driver pointed to a leather pouch on the desk, and Ülle went to it.

'The pink vial, yes?' she said. 'That's the one you need when you haven't moved enough. I remember this, too.'

She opened the pouch to pull out the vial and a syringe. Once she'd half-filled the syringe with fluid, she held it up for Driver's approval before kneeling beside Mormor. He kept his pistol trained on Ülle, ready for treachery. She leaned in to administer the shot, then paused.

'Mormor, you must spare her,' she said. 'Promise, and I'll inject you.'

Driver shouted at her in the other language. Then he stepped closer and pressed the gun into her back. His arm was shaking. 'Just give her the shot,' he said. 'Or I'll shoot you and do it myself.'

Ülle still hesitated. Then she lifted aside a fold of skin on Mormor's arm and slid the needle under it.

They waited and watched. Eventually, Ülle got up to check on the baby. Somehow he had chosen that moment to fall asleep. Driver stayed by Mormor's side, encouraging her to breathe. The heaviness in Regan's legs had started to ease, and the band around her head had disappeared. She considered making a break for it, but when she snuck a glance toward the door, she saw that it was closed, maybe locked, and a long way off. Anyway, she couldn't just leave Ülle.

In time, Mormor sat up and clambered back into her chair. Her breathing grew less laboured. She looked down at her desk, tucked the syringe and vial back into their pouch, then picked up her knitting and started into it again. After a minute, she raised her head, her eyes passing over Ülle and Itzy before coming to rest on Regan. 'Take her back to the storage room,' she told Driver. 'I'll watch these two.'

Regan felt a throb of blood in her ears, and Ülle gave a cry of disbelief.

'You can handle them?' he asked Mormor.

Mormor snorted with contempt.

Regan thought of begging her for mercy. Didn't Ülle helping her just now count for anything? But Regan herself had only sat there, accruing no value.

'Mormor, you must not do this,' said Ülle.

'Don't argue,' said Mormor. 'I'm giving you and Itzy another chance. It's more than you deserve.'

Regan couldn't let Ülle keep putting herself at risk, not for someone who was basically a stranger to her. If Regan wanted to get out of this, she had to speak up for herself.

She cleared her throat, louder than she intended, and suddenly they were all looking at her. 'If you let me go, I won't talk to anybody,' she said. 'I swear.'

Mormor's eyes narrowed, and she waved at Driver to get going.

'Or you could keep me here,' Regan went on, louder. 'I could look after Itzy and the baby. I could do the cleaning. Whatever you want.'

Driver drew closer, pointing his pistol. When he seized Regan by the arm and lifted her from the chair, Itzy gave a long moan.

'Mormor, I beg you,' said Ülle.

Mormor said nothing. Driver sunk a shoulder under Regan's armpit and began to lug her toward the door. Unable to restrain himself any longer, Itzy ran at them. Driver let go of Regan and turned the gun on him.

'Don't shoot,' Regan cried. Her knees buckled, but she kept upright. A second later, Itzy threw his arms around her. She felt his breath tickle her ear as he pressed his nose into her cheek. Standing there, it occurred to her that the air in the room held not the slightest hint of green. Whatever had triggered Ülle's and Itzy's off-gassing must have petered out.

Regan felt hands reaching in to separate Itzy from her. She assumed it was Driver, but once Itzy had been prised away, she saw that it was Ülle.

Ülle ordered Itzy off to the side, then pulled Regan into herself. 'I'll talk with Mormor,' she whispered. 'We'll make it to the sanctuary.'

'I know,' said Regan. It was easier to pretend that she believed it.

The sight of them holding each other was too much for Itzy, who returned to wrap his arms around them. The embrace was Regan's first group hug since she was little. There was none of the stifling heat that she remembered from being sandwiched between her parents, just Ülle's and Itzy's coolness pressing against her in her parents' clothes. Then Ülle held Itzy by the belt while Driver led Regan away.

She wondered where her body would end up. Dumped in the lake, maybe, or mixed into concrete? Her parents would never learn what had happened. Lucinda wouldn't know. All that would be left of Regan would be workout charts, leftovers mouldering in Tupperware, a three-ring binder with her race results. Some shoeboxes full of chintzy trophies. No letters or diaries; nothing to say how she felt about her life. Nothing of four in the morning before the SATS, drunk on sleeplessness, talking Dad down from a high. Nothing of listening to Mom play scales on the piano, years ago, so that one day she could accompany him while he sang. Nothing of all the afternoons Regan had spent massaging her injured foot, knowing it would do no good and in fact only made the stress fracture worse but unable to stop, squeezing until the pain rubbed out her hunger and her fingers cramped.

'Driver, will you not say something?' cried Ülle. 'Will you always do just as Mormor says?'

To Regan's surprise, he stopped and released her arm. Beside them, the liquid in the vat belched and quivered, then grew still, its greenness at odds with the white walls and polished metal surfaces. If not for the glass lid, she wouldn't have been surprised to see a frog kicking across the surface or a dragonfly alighting on the lip.

Driver, too, seemed absorbed by the sight. It was some time before he turned to Mormor, looking sheepish. 'I could move upstairs in the house, and the girl could take the basement,' he said. 'To be safe, we could keep all four of them down there. We could put locks on the doors and windows.'

Mormor gave him a long look. Then she picked up her needles and began to knit.

'It was just an idea,' he muttered, taking Regan's arm again.

'Driver, wait,' said Ülle. 'Can't I at least say goodbye to her?'

This time, he didn't pay her any heed.

Itzy whined, and Regan thought that Ülle might send him charging at them. She couldn't have given up. She must be waiting for the right moment. If she couldn't get Mormor to let Regan go, eventually she'd rescue her from the storage room again.

It was nice to imagine, at least. Regan knew she was kidding herself, though. Mormor seemed to have been living mobster-style for a while now. She wouldn't change her mind, and she wouldn't give Ülle another chance to play the hero.

They were almost to the door when Regan saw Itzy's ball lying ahead of them. 'Hold on,' she said, bending to retrieve it. 'He'll quiet down if he has something to play with.'

She gave it a quick squeeze, then threw it in Itzy's direction, way too high. He stretched for it with Ülle still gripping his belt. Snagging the ball in one hand, he pulled it down and cupped it to his chest, his goofy smile returned. He seemed to live in a moment and then the next with no carry-over. He was probably the one happy grown-up human being in the room.

Regan had this thought, and with a sudden clearness, she realized what she had to do. 'I need to talk with you,' she said, turning to Mormor.

Mormor glanced up from her knitting, a look of tired amusement on her face.

'I have a proposition,' Regan said. 'But I need to tell you about it alone.' If Ülle was in the room, she'd raise objections, try to reason with her, when it wasn't a reasonable situation.

'Alone?' said Mormor. She gave a braying laugh, then returned to her knitting. Driver tugged Regan toward the door.

'Two minutes,' she said. 'That's all I want.'

His hand on her arm was less insistent than it could have been. She was thinking how, once they were out of the room, she might still convince him to let her go, when Mormor spoke again.

'Two minutes,' Mormor said. Still not looking up from her work, she told Driver, 'Take Ülle and Itzy for a walk.'

Ülle seemed reluctant to leave, but Itzy went bounding for the door. As she followed, she stopped to give Regan another hug.

'It will be all right,' Ülle whispered.

'I know,' Regan said. 'You'll take good care of me.'

Ülle looked bemused by these last words, but she didn't have time to say anything. Mormor proclaimed that the two minutes had begun, and Ülle hurried after Itzy and Driver. Once they were gone, Regan heard the click of the door being locked from the outside.

She turned to approach Mormor. Her legs were still wobbly, and the effort of walking without assistance reignited her cough. When she reached the chair across from the desk, she gripped its back to keep herself vertical. Mormor looked her up and down, as if only now properly taking her in.

'Driver tells me you've won medals for running,' Mormor said. Regan wasn't sure if she was making a joke.

'It was a while ago,' Regan said.

Mormor turned her head to evaluate her own arms. For all the loose flesh on them, they were enormous, but Mormor seemed disappointed by what she saw.

'At your age, I was going to be world champion in the shot put,' she said. 'Now here I am in this place.'

She pushed the needles and scarf forward until they were at the edge of the desk. Then, as if suddenly remembering the baby behind her, she stood and lumbered over to peer at him. Apparently satisfied by what she saw, she returned to her chair and leaned across the desk toward Regan.

'Tell me your proposition,' she said.

Regan took a deep breath. 'I want you to flatpack me.'

A glint came into Mormor's eyes, and Regan expected her to laugh, but she only scrutinized her face. 'You are a crazy girl,' she said.

'You can do it, though, can't you? That's what all this equipment's for? People don't need to have the plague to be flatpacked, right?'

Mormor made a tent of her fingers and sank into contemplative silence. Regan began tapping out the seconds on the back of the chair. Thirty went by before she couldn't keep quiet any longer.

'Flatpacking me will make things easier for you,' she said, speaking quickly. 'If you kill me, Ülle will be angry, and Itzy will be a wreck. He thinks I'm his father. If you flatpack me, they'll be happy, and I'll lose my memory, so I'll be guaranteed not to rat you out.'

Mormor closed her eyes. Her head moved slowly side to side, as if weighing one option, then another. 'I couldn't sell you,' she said. 'If the police found you, it would be difficult.'

'So don't sell me. Inflate me, and hide me wherever you're going to hide Ülle and Itzy and the baby.'

'You could turn out to be poisonous,' said Mormor. 'You might live only a week.'

'Maybe. But that could be true for them, too.'

Without speaking, Mormor picked up the tablet from the desk and examined its screen. Regan wondered if the cameras had caught movement, if Ülle and Itzy had tried to escape, but after a few seconds, Mormor set the tablet back down and didn't look at it again.

'If I flatpack you, you might remember things,' she said. 'You could still cause trouble.'

'If I remember things, you can kill me.' Speaking the words, Regan sent a shudder through herself, but Mormor just nodded. 'Besides,' Regan added, 'if you've been having problems with the way you're flatpacking people, wouldn't it help to try again? In case you want to sell your equipment or something.'

Mormor looked pensive, so Regan left her to think. Hobbling to the centre of the room, she peered into the vat. Close up, its green goo smelled of rancid butter. She imagined climbing in, then being crushed by some machine until she was thin as thread. She imagined Ülle blowing into her, feeding her, choosing her clothes. One day, maybe, her memories would return, and she could stop being little more than a kid to her, the two of them happily holed up with Itzy and the baby in Mormor's basement. Even if Regan's brain stayed blank, it might be fine. No more decisions about what to do. No counting miles and calories. No endless bulking and shrivelling of her will to live. Just a smile on her face all day.

Maybe she'd never really hoped to die. This could have been what she'd wanted all the time, except she hadn't known it was an option.

There was a knock at the door, and Mormor called for Driver to enter. He followed Ülle and Itzy back into the room.

'Tell me, is Carel still here?' said Mormor.

Driver replied that he was.

'Then ask him to come in here,' she said. 'There's one more job before he goes.'

Driver left, locking the door behind him. Ülle and Itzy rushed to Regan's side, Ülle's face full of worry and Itzy bouncing on his toes, happy to be reunited with his papa.

'What is going on?' asked Ülle. 'What have you been discussing?'

Regan glanced at Mormor and found her staring back. At the same time, they drew a breath, like they'd planned it that way.

'It will hurt,' Mormor said, almost casually. 'More than anything.'

'That's okay,' said Regan. 'I can take it.'

And she could.

TEN

LULLABY

Tingle of waking. Lips on her neck, their tug and tug. The squelch of air. Life at the bellows, veins flush, elbows thickening. A pop in the ears, a shush, a buzz. Vegetal musk. The deliciousness of being filled, stretched taut, balloon bent on bursting.

Lolling on the cool, hard earth. One mouth, then another, blowing. A trickle through her gullies. The warm wave of Mama's voice, Papa trilling his song. Crack of brightness. Flood of light. The world rushing to her in a blurry freshet. Mama and Papa shifting about her, dark shapes of love.

Apple juice, Regan. Drink the apple juice. Cup in her hands, a careful tilt. Shiver of sweetness. The cold tang inside her.

A prickle on her neck, hard and round, funny to tweak, but Mama says no, little one, don't touch that, no. Come, and I will tell you stories.

Little one totters across the world, and when she looks up, there is Mama! Catches her in her arms. Screams, laughter, giggles. She totters away, and when she looks up, there is Papa! Catches her in his arms. Screams, laughter, giggles. Somewhere outside, in the leafy lull, a creature is howling, sliding high and low, but it is far away. She runs across the world, and when she looks up, there is Mama, catching her in her arms! She wants to do this all the time. She needs nothing more. She'll do it forever if she can.

Robert McGill's writing has appeared in magazines including *The Atlantic*, *The Dublin Review*, *Hazlitt*, and *The Walrus*. He teaches at the University of Toronto. His previous books include two novels, *The Mysteries* and *Once We Had a Country*, and two non-fiction books, *The Treacherous Imagination* and *War Is Here*. Visit him at robert-mcgill.com.

Typeset in Whitman and Gotham.

Printed at the Coach House on bpNichol Lane in Toronto, Ontario, on Zephyr Antique Laid paper, which was manufactured, acid-free, in Saint-Jérôme, Quebec, from second-growth forests. This book was printed with vegetable-based ink on a 1973 Heidelberg KORD offset litho press. Its pages were folded on a Baumfolder, gathered by hand, bound on a Sulby Auto-Minabinda, and trimmed on a Polar single-knife cutter.

Coach House is on the traditional territory of many nations, including the Mississaugas of the Credit, the Anishnabeg, the Chippewa, the Haudenosaunee, and the Wendat peoples, and is now home to many diverse First Nations, Inuit, and Métis peoples. We acknowledge that Toronto is covered by Treaty 13 with the Mississaugas of the Credit. We are grateful to live and work on this land.

Edited by Alana Wilcox
Cover design by Ingrid Paulson
Interior design by Crystal Sikma
Author photo by Fiona Coll

Coach House Books
80 bpNichol Lane
Toronto ON M5S 3J4
Canada

416 979 2217
800 367 6360

mail@chbooks.com
www.chbooks.com